AWAKENINGS
THE CHRONICLES OF NEREZIA - I

AWAKENINGS

Copyright © 2024 Claudie Arseneault.

Published by The Kraken Collective
krakencollectivebooks.com

Edited by Dove Cooper.
Cover by Eva I.
Character Portraits by Vanessa Isotton
Interior Design by Claudie Arseneault.

claudiearseneault.com

ISBN: 978-1-7389259-1-9

The Chronicles of Nerezia

AWAKENINGS

THE CHRONICLES OF NEREZIA - 1

Claudie Arseneault

Kraken
Collective

NEREZIA

(LOWER CONTINENT)

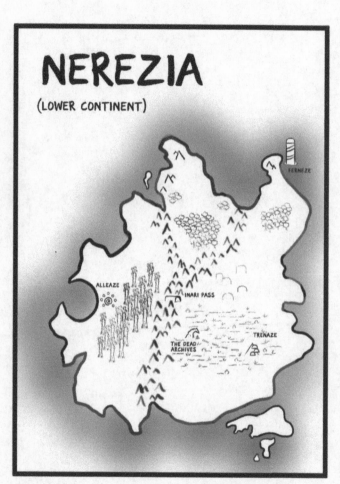

NEREZIA
(LOWER CONTINENT)

FERNEZE

ALLEAZE

INARI PASS

TRENAZE

THE DEAD
ARCHIVES

Horace (e/em), Embo Extraordinaire

Excitable and talkative, Horace has a reputation for failing apprenticeships despite eir best efforts, but plenty determination to keep trying.

Aliyah (they/them), Mysterious Stranger

Left with the strange ability to transform into an eldritch tree and the memory of a mystical forest, the quiet and perceptive Aliyah is on a quest for answers.

Rumi (he/him), Anxious Artificer

Rumi travels the world in a magical Wagon and springs his marvelous creations on the isolated cities of Nerezia. He disguises protectiveness and anxiety under pessimism and grumpiness.

Here is our Hero, ready to begin at last. Only, the Hero is not a Hero, capital letter H yet. They stand in Trenaze's beautiful market, surrounded by the labour of local artisans and craftsfolk, uncertain of their purpose in life, unaware of their origins, and unfit still for the tremendous challenge ahead of them. But that is all right. All it takes is a single event—an inciting incident, if you will—and the forging will begin. It is time. Nerezia needs its Hero.

Archivist Neomi

1
The Grand Market

Just because Horace had failed every apprenticeship in the last fifteen years didn't mean e would fail this one, too.

Or at least, that's what e told emself as e surveyed Trenaze's Grand Market, the weight of eir previous failures pressing harder than the weight of eir official Clan Zestra armour. Watching over the market was eir first real test as an apprentice, eir first day in the field without shadowing a mentor, and every interaction felt like an opportunity to disappoint. E needed to prove emself as a capable member of the clan and earn a prolonged place as a Ka. Horace ka-Zestra sounded great. E wanted that name, wanted to belong so badly the ache in eir lungs turned breathing into a struggle.

Or perhaps that was the sweltering heat. Eir cactus leather breathed well, but it was an additional layer, and combined with the shield on eir back, Horace still sweated eir own considerable weight in water. The desert sun pounded through Trenaze's pink dome, sizzling against everybody's skin and casting a light haze over the covered stalls and their wares.

The Grand Market sprawled at the bottom of the Nazrima Peak, where the roads snaked up towards the city, and formed the core of one of Trenaze's three plateaus. Tents, stalls, and tables were erected in a large dusty area, radiating from a central hub in a spoke-like pattern, with each line assigned a theme. Potential customers climbed down from the city's higher platforms, eager to see what Trenaze's best craftsfolks had to offer, or to discover if any travelling merchants had survived the outdome, bringing in prized delicacies of rare proteins and other wonders from distant cities.

Horace had spent a lot of time here over the years, especially while e had tried out as a dedicated seller. It was the longest e'd apprenticed to a clan before they'd rejected em— for all of Horace's genial nature and love of conversation, eir *convincing* skills never seemed to improve, and in time the clan had recommended e look for a permanent home elsewhere. Despite the failure, Horace loved the market, and the market loved em.

E moved from one tent to another, staying in the shade as much as possible and chatting with the sellers within while e made eir rounds. First was Old Marin and his blossoming flower stand. In the seven years since Horace's apprenticeship with him, the old dwarf had grown even stockier, his beard thicker and richer. He'd woven strings of purple and yellow button flowers within it, matching the garlands all around his stall. Status of his business: *blooming, of course.* And so was Colton's Cobbler Corner, and every old mentor Horace passed by. They greeted em with grins and a slap on the back—

those who could reach that high, anyway—and many wished em well on this new apprenticeship. Horace ignored the doubts laced within their tones, which were all too close to Gavin-der's own when they'd reviewed eir duties this morning.

Eir mentor had been convinced e'd forget them as soon as e got to the market—that e'd notice a cool hat or an old friend and it'd all fly out of eir cracked shell of a brain. Which, all right, Horace *had* talked with Old Marin a fair bit, but e still remembered everything! First e had to spend the morning patrolling the market, ensuring no one got lost or agitated. Eir armour made em a beacon, a source of guidance for those in need. Eir sword and shield, in theory, served as reminders that even in dire circumstances, e was ready to intervene. In practice, Horace prayed to the glyphs e never needed them. E'd spent far longer training hand techniques to disarm and contain, or how to de-escalate a situation to avoiding needing it entirely, than anything with the blade.

E paused to scan the crowd and evaluate, as eir mentors so often had when e'd trailed them on previous outings. Everything looked normal. Market-goers flitted from one stall to another, haggled prices, shared discoveries with one another. No one seemed aggressive. Everyone was safe and happy, and it was eir job to keep them that way.

Eir gaze flicked up, to one of the three pink domes that made this life possible by keeping Fragments out of Trenaze. Several of them hovered above, long metallic shards bathed in golden light. Horace's heart squeezed despite the trusted protection of the shield. E didn't remember Fragments ever being so close and numerous before. Had e never noticed? A lifetime of endless searching for clothes and tools and other things right in front of em had proven e wasn't the most perceptive, so that must be it.

Besides, eir task was to guard the *inside* of the dome. Hunters learned to avoid Fragment attention or deflect their aggression, to survive out in the surrounding desert. And as much as e envied them in their chance to explore the world, even a fraction of it, e didn't relish the thought facing down Fragments. E'd seen the deep cuts a single shard could inflict, had heard the stories of endless possession. Nightmarish stuff. E tore eir gaze away from the hovering shards, focusing back on the task at hand.

Customers, shopkeepers and craftsfolks needed eir attention. E brought years of community knowledge to bear, advising residents on their purchases and redirecting confused crowds towards the proper spokes. Time flew by, hours lost to lively discussions with strangers, and by the time the market filled with the delicious smell of fried eggs, Horace's latent fears had transformed into unbridled enthusiasm. Being a guard was great! E could walk around and talk all day, and eir mere presence served to reassure. Perhaps this *had* been eir calling all along.

Fifteen years of failing—of being Trenaze's eternal apprentice—and e might finally have found eir place. Horace was desperate to escape this limbo, to prove emself *capable* and be treated as a full adult. This might be the one thing e was good at, the one profession with a community waiting for em. E'd know, after this afternoon— or rather, after the one measly hour e'd been assigned to watch the shield dome's majestic glyph. Staying still wasn't eir strength, but *surely* e could manage this short a time.

Eir heart light, Horace strolled eir way towards eir favourite area of the market: the outsider's slice, a slim, triangular open space extending from the market's centre to the edge of the dome's circle, where it met the great, long-deserted trade routes of the world.

With Fragments rendering travel impossible to anyone without protection against possession from them, most of the market was reserved to locals, and there was a certain routine to it, an ebb and flow Horace had long since grown used to. In the thin stretch of the outsider's slice, however? That's where exciting new people settled, rarely more than one or two at any given time, with wares and tales to fill eir head with dreams.

When rumours of a new arrival spread through Trenaze's three plateaus, Horace always made the long trek down from the Upper Terrace to the Grand Market, eager to browse exotic wares and hear the travelling merchants' stories. E'd dream of emself skating over frozen waters with bladed shoes or walking the boardwalks of marsh cities, eir face protected from bugs by a net. They were silly dreams; Trenaze had no clans of explorers or even dedicated merchants. To leave the city was to have failed, to be without the community of a professional trade. But one could always keep dreaming, yeah?

Today's curiosity was a tall wagon-like apparatus, with huge metal wheels, their bronze tint a delightful contrast with the white oak and blue-green shade of the cyanwood in the mainframe. The wood formed four walls then curved into a rounded top along which a long pipe ran, sometimes splitting towards other pipes, cogs, and further eccentricities which combined into an unfathomable mechanism. Some served as support for a platform atop the wagon, a cozy terrace surrounded by metal railings.

A set of tables had been spread in front of the wagon, and the three-foot-tall isixi owner scurried around them, hidden by their wares. Their small claws clicked and clacked with every strange contraption lifted and placed, their yellow reptilian eyes darting through the eclectic ensemble they were putting together. They moved about in quick bursts, their tail whipping the ground at the slightest stop, raising dust and chaos about them. A pair of goggles perched on their head, perhaps as protection against their own whirlwind.

The dust filled Horace's lungs as e reached the table, coating eir mouth so thick e was coughing before e could utter a single greeting. The isixi's head snapped up in eir direction and they scrambled closer.

"Oh no, I'm so sorry, Honoured Stranger! I'm not used to all this desert dust, but we can't have you coughing all around Rumi's Wandering Wagon of Wonderful Wares. A moment."

They hopped onto the smallest of stepladders then rummaged through the mound of gadgets on the closest table. The ruckus was impressive in and of itself, but not quite loud enough to bury Rumi's—and Horace had to assume this was the proprietor, Rumi—triumphant cry.

"I've got it!"

They brandished a strange apparatus, and a staccato of metal cogs echoed across the open marketplace, emerging from a copper horn attached to a wooden box and linen sack. It was all e had time to glimpse before blue glyphs along the horn flared to life, blinding even through the dust, and the air was suddenly pulled towards Rumi and their device, *into it*. Even Horace's coils of hair lengthened, only to curl back when the pull brutally ended. Where once was a cloud of dust now stood a proud Rumi, their clawed hands holding tight to a small box of mechanisms from which protruded the horn. An enormous bag remained attached behind it and bulged with recently captured air.

"Voilà!"

Horace's booming laughter swept through the open space. "Incredible! Did you build that?"

"Certainly did," Rumi declared. "I've got to keep the hands and brains busy on the long road. And I like tinkering."

Horace couldn't imagine *travelling* like that. Eir daydreams always happened *at* destinations, and e'd only left Trenaze's dome shield once, towards the end of eir apprenticeship as a leatherworker, to watch the hunters work and understand the dreadful risks they undertook on behalf of the city. Out in the craggy desert, every flicker of light had left em sweating and terrified of a Fragment attack. Those, too, were conveniently absent from eir longing for the outside world.

"You're alone?" e asked. "All that time and no one to talk to?"

That sounded almost more frightening than the Fragments. Silence always felt like air gathering in Horace's lungs, growing and growing until it threatened to burst out. E needed to talk, loud and often, and not to emself.

"Kind of, yeah." Rumi shrugged then hopped down from their stepladder. "Are you looking for anything? This table is tools, gadgets, toys… Everything I built!" With an annoyed swish of their tail, they added, "And over there's specialty food from all the way over in Cinnize. Can't get that here, for sure."

Most market-goers had cluttered near the second table, huddling over the smoked fish and grilled insects from far away—fancy proteins Horace couldn't afford. The tools were better, anyway. They all looked so complicated! E could spend hours trying to tease out what they were supposed to do, and eir fingers itched to press buttons and turn levers to try them out.

"Can't, I'm afraid." E tapped eir chest, where a triangle barred with three horizontal lines had been embroidered, representing the Nazrima Peak and Trenaze's three main plateaus. "I have to work."

And soon e'd have to stand watch near the glyph.

"Oh, you're part of … what was it, the Clan Zestra?" Rumi asked. "Very noble of you."

Horace squared eir shoulder. "Horace ka-Zestra—so, still in training. E/em pronouns."

The name tasted good on eir tongue. If e could impress Gavin-der enough, e'd make it in more permanently. E hoped the clan would confirm the *ka* in it, that this first trial wouldn't mark the end of eir apprenticeship.

"Just Rumi, of the incredible Rumi's Wandering Wagon of Wonderful Wares. I've been using he/him for well over a decade now." He flexed his knees in a little bow. "I suppose I'll leave you to your watching! You'll make a fantastic guard. I mean, you're what, three times my size?"

Rumi threw his hand up high to illustrate his point, and Horace laughed. "More like two, I'd say."

"It's all the same from down here. Especially for my neck."

Horace wished e didn't have to leave Rumi yet. E wanted to hear of sprawling forests and endless oceans, of underground cities or coastal towns. Besides, it was refreshing to talk with someone who'd no idea how many apprenticeships e had failed before—someone who saw the potential to come, not the one wasted. But if e wanted eir potential recognized permanently, then e needed to prove emself, and eir turn to watch the Shield Glyph at the market's centre had come. With a last goodbye and a deep sigh, e left Rumi's Wagon behind.

The heart of the market was, ironically, the only place devoid of tents and stalls. Here, a large and open area surrounded the dome shield's core, a stone platform a few feet high that extended into an elegant sculpture which wrapped around the Shield Glyph. The glyph was a series of fuchsia lines struck into a giant floating crystal, and it shone a pleasant pink, tinting the dusty ground around in its soothing hue. A single beam of light erupted from the top of the crystal and climbed high in the sky, spreading above everyone's heads in the Market's massive dome shield.

There were *still* a lot of Fragments on the other side. More than earlier, even, and some flung themselves at the barrier. Horace tried to count the swarm of jagged metal and light, but they moved through one another, their form sharper than the usual distant planar distortion you could sometimes spot far away, outside the dome. Why were they so close? Had they grown hungry? Did they hunger? E'd never stopped to ponder Fragments' lives before, if one could call it that. The dangerous shards either attacked living beings outright, or they possessed them, forcing them into a loop of reenacted movements until they collapsed from thirst and exhaustion.

But they hadn't pierced through the domes in decades. It'd be fine. The barrier was holding, as it always had. No need to dwell on horror stories. Horace wrenched eir gaze away again.

Gavin der-Zestra waited for em at the foot of the sculpture, near the only door leading inside. A force field protected the crystal of the Shield, making this one door the only access point—the only point that needed to be guarded.

"I've been waiting." Gavin always managed to impose despite being no taller than Rumi. He had light brown skin and a shock of curls far darker than Horace's own, which framed his bushy, eternally frowning eyebrows.

"I-I'm not late, am I?" Horace glanced at the sky as e jogged the rest of the way, but the Fragments had grown so numerous they hid the sun. Which meant it had to be behind them, so it was fine. E often struggled with time, but e'd been careful today.

"You're not early either."

Was e supposed to be? Horace didn't remember any instructions like that, but perhaps guards arrived early so the shift exchange was finished by the given hour. E wanted to ask, but what if Gavin had told em, and e *had* forgotten? E needed to impress. Questions could wait for later.

"Anything to report, Horace-ka?"

Report meant meaningful information, not a

detailed recounting of eir entire day. E had been taught that very early on. Yet as e reviewed eir morning, the words spilled out of their own.

"There's a new merchant in the outsider's slice! Rumi of the Wandering Wagon of Wonderful Wares! You wouldn't believe all the gadgets he—"

"Horace," Gavin snapped, "unless he is agitating needlessly, I'm not interested."

"N-no! Of course not. He's very kind."

"Yet you chose to report on him instead of the mess above our heads."

Gavin waved an angry finger at the dome, where the flock of Fragments was now slamming into the dome. Horace cringed with every hit, instinctively expecting the Fragments' sharp edges to pierce through the dome as if through skin.

"I had both in mind?"

Gavin frowned at the obvious question mark in eir voice. E should have been firmer. It was true! E *had* intended to ask about the Fragments. It was a relief to know e wasn't the only one disturbed by their number and behaviour.

"Your job now is to stand with your two pretty feet solidly in this doorway and make sure no one gets inside. Nothing more, nothing less. I'll reach out to the hunters to determine what got these Fragments so agitated and what to do about it."

Relief spread through Horace. The hunters would know what to do. They dealt with Fragments in the outdome all the time. E could focus on eir task and guard this door, and stop glancing up every time eir thoughts drifted back to the mass above.

"Not a soul will make it through this door," e promised.

"They better not."

Gavin stomped off, his final warning leaving Horace hot with a tangled mess of feelings — guilt even though e hadn't done anything wrong, and determination that it wouldn't happen, and worry that it always seemed to happen regardless of eir best intentions. E swallowed it all to deal with later. If e got too caught up in eir head, e'd mess up for sure.

From eir position at the foot of the Grand Market's Shield Glyph, Horace still had a decent view of two slices of the market: the outsider's, and Clan Harrera's, with its displays of bright fabrics, brand-new clothes and shoes, rugs and curtains, and other delightful objects woven, knitted, cobbled, and so on. The crowd ebbed and flowed, small groups moving between stalls and chattering away, with the occasional busybody weaving through them, eager to get their chores finished. Many slowed to look up, pointing at the gathered Fragments, frowning. Horace squared eir shoulders and offered eir best reassuring smile at any who then looked eir way. Gavin was on his way. He had this under control. E was not as worried as everyone else, not at all.

Horace glanced towards the mechanical teal wagon where Rumi conducted his business, hoping for a new demonstration to distract em from the tightness in eir chest. Someone new had stepped up to Rumi's gadget table. They leaned forward, dark tattered cloak protecting them from the sun and hiding their face from Horace. The crowd's rumble buried their hushed words, but by their sharp gestures towards the Wagon and the irritated tail flick it provoked in Rumi, none of them pleased the small inventor. He gesticulated as he replied, but the stranger didn't step away or make any calming gesture. They leaned forward, and Horace found emself drifting closer. Just in case.

A flash of pink at the upper edge of eir vision dragged eir attention back up, stopping eir wayward feet before e could leave the door too far behind. The swarm of Fragments smashed into the barrier with more insistence, bouncing off as the dome rippled. Fear threaded through Horace's lungs, tightening them. What would e do if they got through before the hunters came? E had a shield and a sword, but eir training was perfunctory—Trenaze was a peaceful city, and conflicts were resolved through talk or threat far more than actual battle. But e was getting carried away again. Gavin was coming. He was a good guard. Efficient. Fragments had not broken through any of Trenaze's three domes in living memory—eirs, and most citizens, anyway. Nothing would happen.

Nothing, as long as the crystal core and its glyph remained untouched.

A deep sense of foreboding filled Horace, dread coiling in eir stomach and building up to eir throat. Slowly, e turned towards the stone sculpture towering behind em, eir gaze sliding up the walls and to the platform above.

A single figure stood inside the glyph's ward, their visage hidden behind a grinning porcelain mask. An unnatural breeze swept their bright orange cape as they raised a hand, and a dark pink glow surrounded their fingers. The same colour as the glyph.

"Hey!" Horace called.

Despite the panic clogging eir throat, eir shout carried loud and clear. The figure tilted their head, and the cordial grin of its mask sent a shudder down Horace's spine. How had they gotten inside? E'd only taken a few steps, they couldn't have snuck behind Horace, there was no way, was there? But then they'd have had to phase through the Shield Glyph's ward, and if they could do that...

Cold fear doused Horace as the mysterious bastard flicked their wrist, and the glyph behind them—the one thing that stood between the Grand Market and the Fragments outside— flickered.

It vanished only a second, but the effect rippled upward, through the beam of light and the dome, a brief opening. A single second without protection—an eternity for Fragments.

They plunged inside.

2

The Fragmented Amalgam

The Fragments dove inside, a flock of shards catching the sunlight, swirling in a glittering murmur. Their metallic edges caught the pink glow of the dome as it closed above them, reflecting it brightly, tinting the golden hue around them. They flew down in such a tight formation, the light blurred together, a single golden halo around the shards, almost as if it held them together.

No, wait. Horror dropped into Horace's lungs, a heavy rock pushing all breath out. There was no 'almost' there. They were fusing. *Fusing!* When and how in the glyphs had Fragments started fusing?

The thirty or so Fragments melded into a

single entity, a great beast with four legs and two great wings that towered over Horace. Individual shards still jutted out, creating deadly spines and a long, barbed tail, and the 'wings' were two large triangles slowly spinning. The body itself wasn't complete: cracks remained between the original Fragments, held by the golden glow. The creature roared, a horrible screech of a thousand metal pieces grinding against one another.

Below it, the Grand Market's visitors scattered, their horrified screams an echo to the discordant grind.

E wanted to scream, too, but the sound stayed stuck in eir throat, held back by a vague sense of duty. Gavin hadn't returned with the hunters, and a frantic look around the panicked crowd didn't reveal any armed troops rushing in to save the day. Right here, right now, there was only Horace. So e had to do something. Even if this was eir first day, and e'd not trained to defend against Fragments, or trained all that much at all yet, *a monstrosity of fused Fragments had made it into the city.* E drew sword and shield with trembling hands and took eir first step towards the beast. E could do this. E had to—or had to try. E took a second step, then a third, then burst into a full dash, every stride closer to the beast-like fusion of Fragments ratcheting eir fear higher. E was rushing to eir death.

The crowd jostled em, a current of bodies pushing and pressing against eirs as people scrambled to get away. Horace used eir height and muscle mass to steady emself, but at this rate, someone would end up trampled before this amalgam even killed anyone. E raised eir sword and cast eir voice out.

"Everyone, stay calm! Run somewhere safe, but stop shoving each other!"

Eir minimal impact was cancelled out by the fused Fragments landing with an eerie screech, sending dust flying all over the outsider's slice. Horace barely made out the outline of Rumi's Wagon through it, and the isixi's high-pitched voice pierced the surrounding screams.

"The Wagon's safe! Everyone inside!"

He'd hopped on one of his tables and grabbed a long telescopic rod, waving it around. Customers obeyed, pushing and shoving to get through the opened doors, and in the chaos of bodies, the frail stranger who'd been arguing with Rumi was flung to the ground. They landed hard on their back, their hood falling to reveal deep brown skin, the characteristic pointed ears of elves, and a long braid of thick, dark hair. Smelling easy prey, the Fragmented Amalgam pounced in their direction, its long tail rearing up for a strike.

Horace leaped in between, shield raised and heels dug firmly into the ground. The tail smashed into the shield, its pointed end skidding off the metal. The impact numbed eir arm and rattled eir bones, but excitement surged through em. E'd done it. E'd blocked a blow! Horace lowered the shield, still shocked, only to see a deadly paw flying for eir head. E flung emself to the ground, and the whoosh of air close to eir head made eir insides melt in fear. Only instinct got em to scramble back to eir feet, but when the tail swished again, eir shield had remained down. It caught em in the chest and sent em flying, vision darkening at the shock.

Night-time. She stands by a pine, the last tree before the cliff. Above, the sky; a sprinkling of stars shining like fairy dust. Below, the ocean; waves lapping in peaceful quiet. A perfect moment, away from the screams of her home. She breathes in deep, plants the soles of her feet in the earth, and sprints forward. The cliff rushes to meet her.

Pain flared in Horace's arm as e hit the ground, and sunlight blinded em. E skidded and rolled, tearing eir uniform on the dirt and rocks. What… Horace blinked, half expecting the night sky to return. Nothing. Nothing but the burning pain along eir arms and back and the taste of dirt on eir tongue. What had happened there? Was that possession? But then, why was e still emself?

Dazed, e pushed emself back up. The outsider's slice was completely deserted, with most shoppers either long gone or huddling by the wagon, clinging to one another. Rumi had climbed on the roof for a better view, his snout poking through the railing, and a few too-curious customers had joined him. Only the hooded stranger was left on the ground, scrambling backward as the Fragmented Amalgam stalked towards them. Horace searched for eir sword or shield, something—anything—to help em run back into the fray, pointless as it was. The beast's tail already rose, scorpion-like, ready for an attack. Maybe if the stranger rolled away, dodged fast enough and long enough for Horace to join them again…

Instead, they froze. They stopped moving entirely, but not in terror, not judging by the strange rapture softening their expression. Horace's stomach twisted, bile rising through eir throat. The stranger was going to die, and they looked elated about it.

"Watch out!" e shouted, as if eir croaked, breathless call could change anything—as if it had any use besides making em feel like e'd tried.

The stranger did not watch out, nor did they move. They stayed in their trance-like state, lips slightly parted, as the Fragmented Amalgam

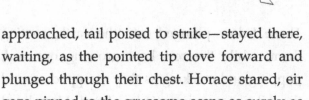

approached, tail poised to strike—stayed there, waiting, as the pointed tip dove forward and plunged through their chest. Horace stared, eir gaze pinned to the gruesome scene as surely as the stranger was to the ground. They spasmed once, coughed. The soft light from the Fragments shone brighter at the tip, growing and growing until tears filled Horace's eyes. E still didn't look away—couldn't.

E was supposed to protect them, and e'd failed.

Guilt surged within Horace, only to flatten with shock as the stranger gasped. They were still *alive*? Their back arched, sliding up on the tail's point for a few bloody inches, and the overwhelming light exploded outward. Horace flinched, shielding eir face against dust and wind with an arm, breaking eye contact for the first time since the strike. When e looked back, the frail stranger had transformed.

Their skin had cracked and thickened into a brown, bark-like carapace, and branches burst in and out of it, running along their arms and legs.

Those below plunged into the earth, rooting them, while the rest kept growing outward, popping and cracking as they wrapped around the tail like one gigantic tree hand. Moss lined the eldritch growth and covered part of their face and hair. Two pale green lights shone where their eyes had been, small dots between the cracks of ancient bark.

The Fragmented Amalgam screeched, and from this close the discordant grind of metal shards sent sharp stabs through Horace's ears, forcing em to eir knees. E bent forward, panting against the pain as the beast tried to yank its tail away. The stranger held fast, pulling themself farther up the jagged tip, their mouth stretching into a smirk with a creak of wood. Horace couldn't have said which of the two was more terrifying.

"Your story is my story," the stranger said, their voice a deep, rumbling chant, each word pulsing with power. "Your pain is my pain. Your joy is my joy. Your life is my life."

The incantation echoed through Horace, a pressure on eir heart and bones rising and falling in time with the phrases, leaving em raw and breathless and ready to surrender. The Fragmented Amalgam buckled forward as if it bowed in response, and the stranger leaned closer and pressed their left palm on its forehead with uncharacteristic gentleness.

"Your story is *my* story."

Their intoned finality was absolute, and Horace would have surrendered everything in a heartbeat if only e knew what to give.

But the Fragmented Amalgam *did* know. The shard under the stranger's palm shone brighter then slowly dissipated into a golden haze. That initial circle spread, and soon the Amalgam's head and shoulders and body vaporized, too, floating above the ground in an almost inviting mist. It swirled around the stranger's arm for a few seconds, a gentle caress, then sank into their skin. The branches followed it, recoiling back into thin arms until only the bark remained— then that, too, was gone.

Then, only a frail elf remained, lips still parted into a dazed half-smile, eyes closed. They swooned, moaned, and collapsed to the ground.

The pressure on Horace's lungs vanished, like a spell unravelling itself and finally allowing em to move. E half-dashed, half-stumbled to the collapsed stranger, eir mind scrambling for all the tidbits of first aid e had learned through eir apprenticeships—as if the dozen burns e'd treated while helping in kitchens would save someone who'd been run through by whatever the Fragment-fusion-stinger-tail had been.

Deadly, that's what it should have been. Any second now, a big pool of blood would spread under the stranger, darkening the orange-tinted dirt. Any... second... Yet when Horace reached the collapsed body, there was still no blood. E dropped to eir knees, turned the stranger over and... no wound either? The only sign of the Amalgam's tail running through them were the tears in their clothes. Horace stared, confused and overwhelmed.

No wound. Their chest rose ever so slightly; they weren't bleeding; they didn't even seem in pain. They'd vaporized an entire flock of

Fragments—something Horace had had no idea was even possible, for hunters or anyone at all—and now they lay there, looking *peaceful*, sleeping.

Horace pinched eir nose, convinced e'd wake up in bed, dawn peeking through the curtains as the sun rose on eir trial day at the Grand Market. This had to be a first-day nightmare. What else could explain Fragments fusing into terrifying beast shapes, or elves turning into eldritch tree beings and dismissing those Amalgams with a touch and a few words, or the echo of power and *rightness* still thrumming in Horace from said words, or the creepy masked intruder who'd started it all?

But e didn't wake up, and with the rush of adrenaline slowly winding down, e felt increasingly nauseated, eir brain a scrambled mess. Somehow, this was real. Eir fingers curled into the stranger's cape, the fabric's texture grounding em, but e kept eir eyes squeezed shut. E could hear the world around moving through the ringing in eir ears—footsteps and shouts, heated discussion, the growing murmur of a crowd.

The scuff of boots near em.

"Holding your nose won't make this mess smell any better." Gavin's sharp tone broke Horace's desperate attempts to keep the world away. E opened eir eyes to find the short guard scowling at em. Gavin dropped his voice to an angry whisper. "Get up. You're supposed to inspire calm and confidence, not be the one barely holding it together."

"Y-yes, Gavin-der."

Gavin grabbed eir wrist as e struggled up, then dragged em farther away from the stranger's body while caretakers swarmed in, small aid kits in hand. Something sharp twinged in Horace's stomach at their approach—jealousy? Fear? Both baffled em, but messed up feelings would be the most normal part of the day. Gavin stopped out of immediate earshot.

"So. Fragments got in, and you were supposed to guard that door. Report?"

"I *was* guarding the door!" Horace tore eir gaze away from the fallen stranger to give Gavin eir full attention. "I barely moved two steps from it. I was there, but someone still got in!"

The masked intruder was long gone, the spot where they'd stood near the Shield Glyph empty. Horace hadn't seen them disappear in the chaos, but their absence didn't surprise em.

Gavin's arched eyebrows didn't inspire confidence. "There is only one way in, Horace-ka. *How* was someone inside the warding field if you never left?"

"I-I don't know. But they were there, with a cape more orange than the sand and a white mask that had this creepy grin. And they did some gesture, and their hand shone, and that's when the shield flickered and the Fragments entered!"

The more e talked, the more Gavin's eyebrows threatened to escape his forehead. Horace petered out, at a loss of what to say. He didn't believe em.

"I swear they were there," e muttered.

"Perhaps. No one in the crowd mentioned them, however, and you're... clearly in shock."

Horace opened eir mouth to protest, but between the latent nausea in eir chest and the way eir thoughts either bumped around eir skull at high speed or vanished entirely, e didn't think Gavin was wrong. Not about the shock, anyway.

"I know what I saw."

"We'll ask about your intruder. Everyone's saying the elf transformed; is that also part of whatever mass fuckery today is?"

"Y-yes."

"Incredible." By his tone, 'incredible' was a far kinder word than what had passed his mind. Gavin-der always sounded annoyed by life itself, but right now he'd achieved a new level of exasperation. "Get your ass back to the headquarters and get a checkup. I heard you fought this thing."

Horace's arm still throbbed where it'd hit em, sending em flying and... hallucinating? With everything else, e'd almost forgotten the strangeness of that, too. "I tried."

"Look, kid." Gavin's tone softened—such a rarity that it lessened the grating reminder that despite eir age, no one would consider em an adult until e locked in an apprenticeship and joined a clan. "You did your best, but your job isn't to get yourself killed. In a panic, you're the beacon of calm, the shepherd. Clan Zestra doesn't deal in heroics and adventures, but in safety."

Horace's gaze flicked back to the Wagon, where Rumi was answering questions from other members of Clan Zestra, gesturing angrily in the stranger's direction. Then it snagged on the elf itself, surrounded by baffled healers, and a deep longing washed over em. Gavin's sharp cough brought em back to the conversation at hand.

"We'll talk about it later," he said. "For now, off you go. Get some rest before Clan Maera swoops in with their questions."

"Clan Maera?"

Horace was too stunned to keep emself from blurting the infamous Clan's name back out at

Gavin, or to keep fear out of eir tone. Clan Maera maintained the three Shield Glyphs that had protected Trenaze for centuries, but unlike other clans, they operated in secret. No one knew what else they did, and their members were held to silence, to be respected and feared. They chose their apprentices, claiming them based on mysterious criteria everyone could only speculate about, and children often whispered tales of one friend or another being snatched in the middle of the night, disappearing for years before reemerging under Maera robes. The shroud of mystery lent itself to exaggerations, and fear, and although everyone was grateful for their work safeguarding the city against Fragments, no one wanted to deal with Clan Maera. But the Shield Glyph had flickered. Of course, they'd want to investigate.

"Don't worry," Gavin said, reaching up to clasp a hand on eir forearm. "You'll get the easy questions. That elf on the ground, though? Wouldn't even be surprised if Maera vanished them."

He said it so casually, but Horace felt cold even in the dry desert heat. E repressed a shiver, wiped eir moist hands on eir pants, and forced emself to nod. Casually nod. Very casually nod. All of this felt wrong in ways e couldn't quite explain yet, but Horace trusted eir guts more than e ever did eir brains. E didn't want Clan Maera to vanish the stranger at all.

"I can carry them to the headquarters."

Eir usually deep voice made a strange squeak, but Gavin let it pass without comment. He ran an exhausted hand through his short hair and sighed.

"Why not? It'd put that bulk and muscles to good use, and I could use all the help I can to get this sorted and reassure people. If the caretakers say they can be moved, you bring them to the headquarters and hand them over to Farina. She'll get them somewhere secure until they wake up and we can have a long chat with them."

Horace offered Gavin another of eir best very casual nods, hoping the frantic beat of eir heart wasn't as loudly audible as it felt. It was likely as credible as eir faked surprise when the caretakers said the elf appeared devoid of wounds, but everyone seemed too busy to pay attention to eir poor lying skills. Horace scooped the stranger from the ground, nestling their thin and wiry body against eir chest, and slowly moved away from the crowd.

Clan Zestra deals in safety, Gavin had said, but he hadn't cared for this stranger's safety at all, even though they'd saved them all, dissipating the Fragments. It felt wrong, to hand them over and let the mysterious Clan Maera interrogate them, or whatever else they did.

As Horace's boots scuffed the sand dusting the streets of Trenaze's lower dome, e recalled its gritty feel under eir palms as e knelt in the middle of the Grand Market, rapt attention on the eldritch tree being facing off a giant fused Fragment. Terror had given way to fascination, pulled out of em by the same force that had spellbound em to the grating tree voice and its incantation. *Your story is my story*. It felt like a dream—not a nightmare, not that part, despite everything—and its echoes wrapped within em now. It had felt *right,* the same way carrying this stranger did now, like e'd found where e was meant to be.

Horace wanted to understand why, wanted to feel that again. E'd never get a chance if Clan Maera took this stranger away. Instead, e'd be the recruit who'd been stationed at the glyph's door when it'd flickered, who'd reported an impossible orange-caped intruder no one else had seen, who'd chosen heroics over safety. Gavin had promised to talk more later, and after enduring over a dozen rejections, Horace had a good idea what that discussion might entail.

Today was a disaster, but for a few seconds in it, it'd felt like eir life had found its axis. E refused to abandon that, not for an apprenticeship e'd likely already lost. Horace stopped long before e reached the mechanical elevator that'd bring em up to Trenaze's midway plateau and Clan Zestra's headquarters. Eir grip tight around the thin body in eir arms, e changed path, to find a refuge where they could recover quietly, away from Clan Maera—and where e could ask eir own questions first.

3
The Stranger

Varena would not be pleased.

Eir friend would be at the Table Hooves by now, getting her establishment ready for the evening, and Horace couldn't think of anywhere else to go where e wouldn't be tracked down immediately. Varena and em had gotten close when e'd worked with her for a few months, cleaning out rooms, hauling fresh water from inside the Nazrima Peak, and obeying her every order—another apprenticeship eventually chalked up as a failure. Neither eir memory of clients' demands nor eir note-taking skills had improved with time, and e had kept starting tasks and leaving em unfinished, distracted by another on the long list of things to do. Varena had kept calling em a friend after e'd been told to find another clan, though, and her business dealt in privacy and quiet moments together, which e needed tonight.

The Table Hooves catered to companions seeking time together away from their respective clans and the large, shared living spaces where one was expected to entertain any and all questions regarding their crafts, or share the day's work with others. While duty would always be to the Clan first, it was well understood that pairs and polycules needed time alone, especially if they belonged to separate clans. A reservation to Clan Viella's many similar establishments was respected as a time of respite and intimacy. Some stayed a night, others several, and during eir apprenticeship here Horace had been instrumental in maintaining their tiny piece of private joy.

As e knocked again, harder, it occurred to em it was a strange place to bring an unconscious stranger to, and eir cheeks flushed at the potential misreading there. E could explain when they woke. This place had excellent food and discrete rooms, e knew the owner, and e had absolutely no intentions for anything sexual or romantic. Working here had taught Horace a lot about what people got up to, and e'd learned quickly that projecting emself in that sort of intimacy left em with a deep unease—like a vise around eir lungs and a numbness in eir brain. E didn't need sex, and e didn't *want* it either. Least of all with this poor stranger who'd had an even worse day than em.

What e did want was for Varena to answer before too many passersby noticed em, so e rapped impatient knuckles a third time. It earned em a gruff call, muffled by the thick door.

"I'm coming, calm down!"

Horace relaxed, eir friend's familiar voice a balm on eir soul—even if it'd turn argumentative soon enough. E listened to the clop-clop of her hooves as she approached the door and prepared eir plea.

Welcome shade beckoned from inside as Varena opened, only to be blocked by her massive form. She was of a similar height to Horace, with the thick thighs so common to munonoxi people. The sunlight conferred a paler tone to her russet fur, which covered most of her body and stretched into a beard at her chin. The latter shivered with irritation as she beheld the scene before her—Horace, still battered from the market fight, eir leather armour scuffed from the tumble on the ground, an unconscious stranger in eir arms. The slit of her rectangular pupils narrowed.

"Really, Horace?"

"I need a room," e pleaded. "I know you always have some set aside."

"They're for members of my clan," she reminded em flatly.

That stung. Friends or not, e should've known the clan duties always came first. E fought through eir sinking feeling.

"Any… others?"

"Doesn't Clan Zestra have resources you could use?"

Hope sprang back, easily revived. That wasn't a *no*. When she stepped aside to let em in regardless, e followed with a skip in eir steps. The back door led into a small kitchen area, and none of the night's cooks had arrived yet. They'd be here soon, ready to start prepping food for the evening, as Horace had for months.

"I need somewhere private. And, hum, for you not to tell anyone."

Her hooves stomped loudly as she stopped and turned around, pointing an accusing finger eir way. "You're bringing trouble to my door, aren't you?"

"The trouble's over."

That was true, wasn't it? The Fragments were gone, and calm would be returning to the Grand Market. That e'd lied to eir mentor and never gone to the headquarters wasn't *trouble*, right?

"You're a terrible liar," Varena pointed out.

"Please," Horace pleaded, staring with the widest, most innocent eyes e could. "I just want them to wake somewhere quiet and private."

She rolled her eyes—a quick tilt of the horizontal pupils—and sighed. "I hate that face, Horace. You can have a spare room, but if trouble does come knocking, it's *your* responsibility."

"O-Of course!"

"And once you're done with whatever this is—" She gestured at the stranger in eir arms, "—you come have a drink and tell me about it."

"Promise," e said. "You're the absolute best, forever and always."

"And don't you forget it," she said. "Take the second room on the left. And since you want it so badly, get it ready yourself."

Horace grinned at the curt order. She'd always covered fondness with gruff orders, setting em to one task or another whenever e'd get too mushy on her. E let the familiarity ground em in this whirlwind of terrifying events and set to work.

Afternoon trickled by, and the stranger slept still.

They didn't twitch or toss, or snore or moan—

didn't give sign of life save for the slow rise and fall of their chest. Horace first paced the silent room, then gave them another once-over despite the caretakers' earlier attention, and finally returned to the pacing, unable to sit still. The more time e had to unwind, the more terrifying and baffling today became.

Horace fought the eeriness the best way e knew: with food. Varena had a great talent for spice and texture, and tonight she'd simmered bell peppers, onions, and mushrooms into a paste of tomato and herbs, then cracked several eggs to cook into it. E had devoured two plates one after the other then left a third for the stranger, expecting them to wake up to the delicious, spicy scent of a hot meal. They hadn't.

Hours had passed and Horace had stayed, the room's silence more and more oppressive. Despite eir best efforts, e mentally reviewed the day, turning the events in eir head every which way. E didn't understand any of it—not the intruder behind the Shield Glyph's protective ward, not the Fragments fusing together into a single entity, not this stranger shapeshifting into a tree-like monster, not the power of their words and how it had rooted em, and certainly not eir burning desire to stay with them, talk to them, protect them. Horace was used to confusion—e tended to be the last one to understand any given thing—but e didn't think others would fare better. Worse, probably, considering Varena had once called em an obtuse optimist.

E was still mulling it over when—finally!—the stranger stirred. They gasped, and their eyes fluttered open, and for a long time they only stared at the ceiling, unmoving. E should have given them time to recover and get their bearings, but after hours of silence, the few extra minutes were too much to ask.

"You're awake!" E sprang to eir feet and leaned over the bed, close to their face. "Hello."

Their lips parted, and wow, Horace hadn't noticed how dry those were. But everything about this stranger felt that way: bone thin and desiccated, like plunging them in water would be the best thing to happen to them. Only their eyes didn't have that sickly, undercared for look. Black and deep and alert, they stared at Horace with obvious wariness.

"Stay back," they said.

Horace realized just how close e'd inched and straightened all the way back with an awkward laugh. "Sorry, didn't mean to scare you or anything! You've just been asleep so long. Hours! I got excited." E ran a hand through eir curls and offered eir best non-threatening grin. They didn't seem reassured. "I'm Horace ka-Zestra. We fought those Fragments together?"

"You… are the fool who jumped in," they said. "I am… Aliyah."

They'd said the first without any judgment, as a simple statement of fact. And it was true. E *had* jumped in.

"That's my duty! Jumping in, I mean, except, er—my mentor disagreed after and said I shouldn't have, but no matter. It worked out, didn't it? After a fashion. I mean, we're both alive, and so is everyone else." E needed to stop rambling, but it was like all the words e'd held in while watching over them in silence now sprung forth. "I don't know about you but that was the wildest day of my entire life."

"Where am I?" they asked. The focused question was a kindness of its own.

"At the Table Hooves. It belongs to Varena der-Viella and she's a friend, so don't worry. We'll be fine. I brought you here after you collapsed. Are you feeling all right? The caretakers said you didn't need medical attention but they've never seen anyone like you either..."

Aliyah's frown interrupted eir ramble. They very slowly pushed themself up to a sitting position and scanned the room. Silence stretched between them, and Horace put all of eir meagre willpower into keeping eir mouth shut. Clearly, they were not inclined to talk. It must have been a lot for them, too, the whole tree transformation and making Fragments dissipate.

"I need to leave."

They slung their legs over the side of the bed. Horace laughed and grabbed their minuscule shoulder. "Leave? Is your egg cracked? You stayed knocked out for hours. You gotta rest, not leave."

E wasn't even finished and Aliyah already shook their head. "Release my shoulder."

Well now. Not even a 'please'? Horace pouted. "That's a no from me. I'm not letting you walk out without a proper meal and full introductions. You haven't even given me pronouns yet!"

The quirk of Aliyah's eyebrows changed, and while they weren't the most expressive, Horace chose to interpret that as confusion. Or thoughtfulness? Perhaps they were considering the offer!

"The default here is they/them, is it not? That is sufficient for me."

"Well, I use e/em." Horace released Aliyah's shoulder, but only long enough to grab the plate and shove it on their lap. "Now you eat. I bet transforming into a tree monster leaves you ravenous. Is that why you're so thin? Not eating after you unleash all that power?"

"A—"

Aliyah clamped down on their question before it could escape then stared at Horace, long and hard. Was that supposed to intimidate em? Stinky eyes rarely induced guilt or shame in Horace unless the feeling already existed. It definitely did not right now, so e only grinned back in challenge. Aliyah twitched, but their expression remained as unreadable as that masked intruder's. Moreso, even—that porcelain mask had had the creepiest of grins.

"Fine," Aliyah eventually whispered, the word almost a sigh. "I will eat if you tell me what happened. From the start."

They wanted em to talk? Horace clapped eir hands, a surge of excitement piercing through the hazy fear of the day. "Now *that* will be my pleasure."

E launched emself into the tale with great gusto, eir booming voice painting first the image of a typical busy market day, all inhabitants safe under the dome shield until a flamboyant masked stranger shattered the peace. Aliyah ate with extreme slowness, one tiny fork at a time, paying more attention to the meal than to Horace. Maybe the story was only a pretext to keep em busy, but Horace had needed to pour the whole tale out to someone who wouldn't scold em for any mistakes, and to give voice to how confusing and terrifying it had all been. Every word out of eir mouth made em feel lighter and steadier.

E spied for a reaction as e reached Aliyah's transformation into a deadly tree being, but they remained stone-faced. They did stop eating, as if bottling any feelings left no energy for anything else. Horace wished people wouldn't do that. E never saw the point in keeping yourself a mystery—how was someone supposed to make honest connections that way? Not that e could've done it if e tried. Eir inability to keep emotions hidden—irritation and panic included—had contributed to eir dismissal as a Clan Viella apprentice.

By the time e finished, Aliyah *had* grown agitated despite their best efforts. The plate lay cleaned out on the bedside table, and their hands clung to one another on their lap. They didn't look at em, only at the door, but the tapping of their fingers on the bed betrayed them. Horace, in a feat of exceptional patience, waited for them to react to the story on their own.

"And everyone saw this?" they asked.

"Everyone around the outsider's slice. Most people had fled, but those hiding in Rumi's Wandering Wagon must have watched those fused Fragments and prayed to the glyphs the Wagon was as safe as promised. They, huh, definitely reported everything to my mentor, who thought Clan Maera would want to ask you questions."

"Right."

A single word, and more silence. Horace had expected a stronger reaction to the mention of Clan Maera, but e was quickly learning that 'strong reaction' wasn't part of Aliyah's normal range. Maybe they didn't fear the mysterious clan the way most people did. Could they be part of it? But they hadn't given any clan affiliation, and they spoke with a lilting accent that'd made Horace believe they'd not lived in Trenaze for long. E wondered what drifted through Aliyah's mind when they got this quiet and intense.

"How late does the market stay open?" they asked.

"Till sundown." Horace glanced at the flitting light through the window. "Two hours, at most? Probably less."

"Once it closes, it is mostly deserted, yes?"

"There might be a few drifters here and there, and the occasional merchants who forgot something or wanted to get prepared for the morrow, stuff like that. Oh, and I suppose there might be others from Clan Zestra around tonight. But no crowds."

Aliyah inhaled, deep and slow, then set the plate aside, back on the bedside table. Their next words seemed to cost them.

"You can take me there. As a guard. Get me where I need to."

They didn't phrase it as a question, and Horace decided that was as good as permission.

E grinned. "Sure! But, huh, there's nothing in the market at that time."

"The Wagon will be there."

The Wagon. They could only mean one thing. "Rumi's Wandering Wagon of Wonderful Wares? But… Why?"

"It can take me out of the city."

A twinge of regret pulled at Horace's stomach. E didn't want them to go, to leave Horace without answers and a cartload of consequences—disobeying orders and showing up without the mysterious tree-shapeshifting elf would not go well on eir record. E swallowed hard, trying to find the courage to prod Aliyah with eir questions.

"I'm glad you're planning on sticking around at least a few hours. Rest is good, you know. Whatever all that was today, it was *a lot*."

"Yes, one could say that."

One could, but *they* didn't? Did this count as a normal day for them? It hadn't even happened to em, for the most part, and e'd needed double the dinner to force a semblance of normalcy on it. E couldn't have stayed calm, had *e* transformed into a destructive tree and vaporized a Fragment flock. Aliyah's aloofness was all the more remarkable for it. Maybe this often happened to them, and they knew all about it. E had to ask about today. And once one question came out, the others followed.

"So ... did you know that orange-caped person? How does the tree transformation work? Have you seen Fragments fuse before? When you touched them..."

E trailed off. With every new question, Aliyah's expression closed off and their frown deepened. Their answer came through gritted teeth.

"I did not know. Not about your intruder, or about the Fragments." Aliyah closed their eyes, and for a brief moment their unreadable expression turned into exhaustion. They masked it quickly. "I would rather not discuss it any further."

"But do you think it's safe now?"

"It's your dome. I do not know whether it will fail you again."

A dozen more questions pressed at Horace's lips, but e held them back. The hunters and Clan Maera had been alerted now, and they could take care of the Shield Glyphs and any Fragment intrusion. E didn't want to tire Aliyah any further, and if they didn't have the answers regardless… Prying felt like forcing them to relive the difficult afternoon. They *had* been run through by that tail-like fragment. What were confusing and scary memories for Horace probably came closer to traumatic ones for Aliyah. Perhaps e could try again, later.

"All right," Horace said, boxing eir worries and curiosity neatly in eir brain for now. "I'll get the saira boards from downstairs."

E was already halfway to the door when e noticed Aliyah's mouth had opened in a small 'o', and although they'd not voiced it, their confusion was, for once, easy to read. Horace grinned.

"Oh, I love new players!" e exclaimed, and left it at that.

E hummed all the way to the storage area,

where e snatched a bottle of cactus wine in addition to the game. Varena could scold em later for not asking—she was nowhere around, and Horace would pay her back.

Aliyah had slid out of bed by the time e returned and started the fire. Nights could get cold, and with the sun rapidly vanishing, heating up the room was a good call. Plus, Aliyah was all bones and no fat—no protection to speak of. Horace liked that they were making themselves comfortable. It made it easier to pretend they'd all had a normal day.

"Got everything we need to kill time until the market's empty. You drink?"

"I—yes."

Their hesitation gave Horace pause. "It's fine if you don't. Either tonight or ever. I'm not big on it in general, but this wine's sweet on the tongue."

They stared again, that long and silent stare, an entire world hidden behind inscrutable black eyes. This stare ended with the hint of a smile, a shy curve of their lips that sent Horace's heart flip-flopping.

"I have simply never tried, but I would like to."

"Oh, I see! Well, you're in good hands."

Aliyah wouldn't be the first newcomer to alcohol e'd initiated. As the oldest resident of the Clan Nissa Nursery—the only one far past twenty years of age who'd yet to find a clan that'd accept em—e'd helped plenty of younger relatives sneak in their first drink over the last years. Many a smarmy teen who'd called em a loser for eir failed apprenticeship had come back crawling for easy access to distilled agave or cactus wine. First, they blessed eir inability to hold a grudge, then they cursed em for insisting e stayed nearby. But at the end of the night, e was picking up drunken bodies and ensuring everyone got to bed safely.

Horace retrieved two small cups of clay then settled on the ground with the game. Aliyah joined em as e served the first drinks, quietly studying eir every movement. When e was done, they wrapped thin fingers around the clay cup and sniffed it. Their nose wrinkled, and the flash of surprise across their face was the most expressive Horace had seen them yet. E laughed.

"Wait until you taste it," e said, before tilting eir glass towards Aliyah and taking a sip. The wine went down, sweet and fresh with a citrus aftertaste that masked some of the alcohol's kick. Only *some* of it, though—and certainly not enough for Aliyah. They startled at the first gulp, shaking the whole of their shoulders and head as they leaned back, their eyes watering.

"What—"

Horace's booming laugh filled the entire room, and to eir delight, Aliyah joined with a quiet chuckle. Warmth coursed through Horace at the discreet sound, calming and inebriating in a way no alcohol could be. It felt *right*, a balm on the stress of the day, and Horace knew e'd seek it out again, the way e so often did friends' laughter. Aliyah wiped their mouth and set down the glass.

"I believe I will take it slow," they declared. "Teach me your game."

Horace complied with great enthusiasm.

Saira had only a few key rules: you had to place dice of four different colours on your board, filling it as fast as possible while respecting the four-by-four layout under. Certain dice combinations granted special abilities—stealing from your adversary, switching dice on your board, placing two—and allowed for interaction between players. Points were counted according to the top of the dice, but the best abilities were always created with lower value dice. Horace had played countless games with Varena, and when e had apprenticed with Vellix, a woodcarver, e'd also painted a plethora of new four-by-four boards to liven up the potential combos.

Aliyah paid careful attention to the instructions, absorbing the rules like the dusty ground after a rainfall. They didn't ask questions, only soaked it up until they declared themself ready. Horace rolled the first set of dice, and they started selecting a die from the pool and placing it, turn by turn, until a new pool needed to be rolled. Aliyah kept quiet, playing each of their moves with utter seriousness. Not drinking, not chatting; only playing. By the time the game ended, Horace was far ahead in points, but Aliyah's eyes shone with determination as they tallied the dice. They lifted their head to meet Horace's gaze, and the shy smile returned.

"I was not ready," they concluded, "but *now* I am."

They grabbed the cup of cactus wine, downed it in one shot, then set it back down gently on the floor. Horace looked on, horrified, as they snatched up the dice bag and rolled the first pool of the game.

"Your move," they said.

No move could have saved Horace that second game. Aliyah turned into a ruthless saira player, chaining powers in unexpected ways and prioritizing combos with which they could destroy Horace's board. The sudden wine intake didn't make them more talkative, either. They studied the board with bright eyes, alert and smiling but silent, always silent—unlike Horace, who could not help but think every one of eir moves out loud, giving away much more than e should. E lost that first game, then the next, before e started countering Aliyah's swift and deadly tactics more effectively. E'd never been a defensive player before—that had been Varena's primary strategy—but against this new foe, Horace had no other choice.

E loved the challenge, and clearly so did Aliyah. They played several games, stretching their fun well past the intended two hours. Horace did manage to win again—once—but Aliyah had em outmatched. Watching them glow silently with every combo was more rewarding than any victory.

Unfortunately, the outside world ruptured their gentle bubble with sharp knocks at the door. Aliyah's dark eyes narrowed as they stared at it, leaving Horace with the distinct impression they didn't want em to answer. But in an establishment like this, only Varena would knock, and only with good reasons. Quiet dread settled in the pit of eir stomach as e cracked the door open. Varena stood on the other side, her arms crossed and clearly very crossed herself.

"You wouldn't believe the stories I'm hearing in the common room, Horace." Her tone could've sliced fingers. "What a day the Grand Market has seen, huh?"

Eir cheeks burned immediately. Of course, she'd hear about the Fragments from customers as they streamed through. Nothing like this had happened in Trenaze in ages.

"Varena, I—"

She stopped em with a sharp raised hand. "I knew you were underselling whatever glyph-cursed mess you'd stepped in when I let you in. But whatever plan you think you have, hiding here, it's a bad one. This is bigger than you, Horace. Let the Clans handle it."

She was right. Somewhere in eir tiny mind, e knew she was right and e should've brought Aliyah to Clan Zestra's headquarters to let others investigate and whatnot. But it had felt wrong then, and it felt even worse now, having met Aliyah, quiet and sharp and closed off. If they hadn't wanted to answer eir questions, they'd have hated Clan Maera's even more—and somewhere between watching them dissipate the Fragments, caught in the sheer gravitas of their presence, and playing silly board games and listening to their soft laugh as they destroyed em, Horace had locked emself into an undeniable, unyielding loyalty. E cared. E cared more than was reasonable, and e didn't have the heart to question it.

"They needed a night to rest. You've heard the story! Anyone would need a night after that."

Varena huffed, her nostrils widening as hot air blew into Horace's face. "Just a night. If the two of you are still here tomorrow, I'll get Clan Zestra myself."

"We won't. I-I promise."

The promise burned eir tongue. Varena meant for em to go to Clan Zestra, not leave, and e hated the omission. Varena's immediate frown didn't help any. She could always tell.

"Tomorrow, Horace," she said. "For your sake."

She clomped away before e could dig emself further into eir own hole, and e closed the door as slowly as e could, before turning to Aliyah. They hadn't moved, but when they spoke, their voice was fierce and resolute.

"I'm leaving tonight. Thank you for showing me this game. It was very pleasant. But we should go."

They stretched, and as they unfolded the weight of the world returned to their shoulders, and to Horace they seemed frail and worried once again, a flower bloom closing in on itself. The sudden pang of loss and regret overwhelmed em.

"Take it. The game, I mean," e said. Aliyah's brows shot up, their mouth twisting to protest, so Horace quickly gathered it up, storing the boards back into the black dice sack. "I'm serious. I can carve and paint another, but you'll never find unique saira boards like these. Varena and I created them."

Aliyah still didn't extend their hands, so Horace shoved the bag into their chest and let go, forcing them to catch it. They gasped and clutched it close. Their lips parted an instant, but whether to protest or thank em, Horace would never know. Aliyah instead nodded, then stored it in the minuscule knapsack they'd had on them before the attack.

"To the market, then."

4
The Wagon

For the first time in eir life, Horace wished e could conceal eir face. If details of the market attack had reached Varena's establishment, near the elevator connecting the Grand Market's lower dome and the upper one, everyone down here would have heard. And they might very well be talking about the poor, ever-failing apprentice who'd been caught in it all. Gavin would have realized e'd never gone to the headquarters by now, too, and eir public status might have gone from 'poor unfortunate soul' to 'potential saboteur'.

This had really been a mistake, hadn't it? Eir steps slowed as panic mounted in the pit of eir stomach, and e struggled to find the sense of righteousness that had changed eir course from Clan Zestra's headquarters to the Table Hooves this afternoon. What had e been thinking? E had one chance at this apprenticeship, and for all of Gavin's gruff reproaches and general eagerness to catch em failing, he'd seemed almost concerned for Horace. E'd let superstition and impulsive kindness take em over, and e'd ruined eir life for a stranger.

At least e was out of Varena's hair. E'd left her a short apology note, a simple *"I'm sorry. You are still the best."* to which e should have added "you are always right and I should listen more", but it was too late for that.

"Horace?"

Aliyah stepped up next to em. E'd stopped walking entirely, and they peered at em from under their hood, silent and inquiring. E could *still* bring them back to the guards. They'd rested now, at least.

"You are having doubts," they said. "Your face is very easy to read."

Horace choked in surprise, but e felt instantly better, having it out in the open. It was always better to talk about things. "I am. My people... I'm sure they'd love to talk to you. This afternoon was very scary for the city. Our dome never fails."

Aliyah pressed their lips together, and turned towards the market's general direction. For a moment, Horace thought they'd say nothing more, but after a few seconds of heavy silence, their shoulders slumped. "I promise I do not have answers for them. I want to leave to seek them, however."

They could be lying, but Horace found that e believed them. Every word, every frown, every refusal to speak. E believed Aliyah's promise, believed they had never seen the masked intruder, believed they wanted answers of their own. They didn't feel like a stranger, but like a friend long lost, one e needed to get to know again. And Horace helped friends in need.

Eir panic receded, solidifying into resolve, and e started off again, keeping to the streets instead of crossing the open market space until they were as close to the outsider's slice as they could.

Most tents and stalls of the Grand Market had been abandoned, their offerings stored and locked away for the night. The silence, so contrary to the day's chirpy bustling, unsettled Horace. The market was meant to be alive, thriving with the chaos of Trenazian life as people hawked and haggled and went about their business. This windswept immobility felt like death, and the pinkish glow of the shield dome above no longer guaranteed safety. Horace kept glancing at it, then at the central structure with the Shield Glyph. No strangers with porcelain masks appeared, but several guards now made rounds near it, in addition to the two at the door.

Rumi's Wandering Wagon had thankfully moved to the very edge of the outsider's slice, where it met the road, and thus away from the central Shield Glyph and the extra guards. Light streamed out of a tiny window on the side, casting its golden glow on the reddish dust.

Instead of striding to the door, Aliyah sidled up to the Wagon's side and pressed their palm against it. Their eyes closed, and tension bled from their expression, smoothing the tight lines of their mouth and lowering their shoulders. Horace watched, confused. They acted like touching the Wagon brought them relief—like jumping into the Underlake after a whole day in the beating sun.

"What—"

The door creaked open and three small steps lowered to the ground. Aliyah released the Wagon and moved towards the beckoning inside light, stopping on the bottom step.

"Thank you for the escort, Horace ka-Zestra," they said.

A deep pit opened inside, eir stomach plummeting down. Was that it? They'd climb inside and leave the city, and Horace would never hear of them again—never hear their quiet chuckle, or understand any of today. E'd get dismissed as a member of Clan Zestra, or worse. Probably worse. Horace didn't want to reach that part of eir life just yet.

"Wait!" E scrambled for a reason Aliyah should wait, something, anything. "Won't Rumi..." Rumi what? E didn't know Rumi. E'd had a quick chat with the isixi before the disaster and seen him argue with Aliyah, but that was the extent of eir knowledge. "I'll leave once I know Rumi won't throw you out."

"And I *will* throw you out," a sharp voice interrupted.

Rumi stood in the golden light, scowling, and instead of the thick, copper-lined glasses on his head, he had a night bonnet. Even with the extra height from the steps, he was barely tall enough to glower down at Aliyah. Hostility sparked between them, so tangible Horace couldn't help but step forward to defuse it.

"We're not looking for trouble, Master Rumi," e said.

"Oh, I know that. You all want a ride."

You all. Horace froze. Em too? E wanted a ride? No, no, e'd only meant to escort Aliyah... right? But if e followed, e could get the answers to today's events. E could even bring them back to Trenaze, return with a success to eir name. Eir gaze swept over the strange wagon again, with its cyanwood structure and hundred tinkered wonders. What was the inside like, e wondered? What *did* it feel like, to travel the world, see the landscape change with the miles, move between the bubbles of culture that had been left across Nerezia? The sheer scope of the possibilities lost em in a labyrinth of daydreaming broken only by Aliyah's sharp voice.

"Your Wagon opened its door for me."

Rumi's teeth clacked. "It's been a bit of a bother recently."

"Recently."

Aliyah infused all of their natural gravitas into the word, as if it held the entire world's meaning, and Rumi stared back, the twitchy sweeps of his tail betraying his agitation. Horace beheld the silent battle, the pressure to talk increasing with every passing second. Aliyah saved em, their tone dropping to a soft whisper.

"It knows me, does it not?" they asked Rumi.

He huffed, then threw his arms up in

surrender. "Yeah, okay, all right! It knows you, or *of* you. Won't leave me alone about it." He stomped down, glaring at the wood under his feet. At the Wagon.

It. Aliyah touching the Wagon. Rumi stomping at it. They kept talking about the Wagon like it was alive and had opinions.

"I don't understand," e said, interrupting the beginning of another silent staring contest.

Rumi startled at eir voice, as if he'd forgotten Horace was there at all. He cast a nervous glance about the market. "Everyone inside."

Everyone included em, yes? Excitement bubbled within Horace. E'd get to see what other inventions Rumi had hidden inside.

And inside, it turned out, was a wonder of its own.

The Wagon opened up, bigger than possible, its roof arching several feet above Horace's head—high enough to allow for a low, second floor in half of it, with a ladder going up. Yet all the inside space didn't make the Wagon *spacious*. Not when every surface, horizontal and vertical both, had been filled up. The outside pipes climbed up, running across the ceiling and towards the second floor and a closed off room, in addition to going through the wooden top to poke outside. They passed through boxes at times, and one led to a big glass sphere in the middle of the ceiling which diffused a soft warm glow.

This main area had a long two-seater, a central table, and a small kitchen counter covered in a mix of plates and gear-filled instruments, dirty with a mix of the last meal and oil stains. Somewhere under the pile, Horace thought e spotted a spiral burner the likes of which e'd seen in the rare, fancy eateries of Trenaze. It'd have to be cleared out to use, or risk setting the whole Wagon on fire—which, if the licks of black on the cyanwood behind it were any indication, had happened in the past.

Most of the space, however, was dedicated to Rumi's workshop—Horace saw no other way to describe the U-shaped table under the second floor, near the front of the Wagon. It held countless instruments to measure, cut, weld, carve, or glyphs knew what else. Crates under it contained a mishmash of materials, and various metal tools seemed stuck to a long band on the wall nearby. Wood shavings covered the entire floor. The pole of a heavy dark teal curtain ran across the wagon to cut off the crafting section if needed, and Rumi pulled it shut as they entered, hiding his current projects.

"The Wagon's magical," he said, as if the space being at least twice as big on the inside hadn't given that part away. "It's… somewhat sentient, and has become more so when I got here."

"So it talks?" Horace asked. That sounded so cool! What kind of voice did a wagon even have? Deep and scratchy? Creaking?

"It's more like… strong feelings. Images, sometimes. No one else has *ever* 'heard' it, or felt it," he added, turning to Aliyah, his reptilian eyes narrowing. "I don't know who you are, but I had a nice, quiet life before it got obsessed with you. Smashing cupboards shut, refusing to help me, pressing the whole feeling of *you* somehow in my head. I don't like it being like that. Can't be healthy."

Horace wondered how much of Rumi's wariness of Aliyah was born from protectiveness for the Wagon. Aliyah pulled their cloak tighter at the accusation, lips pressed tight together. Closing themself off and bottling it all again, Horace thought, and a wave of chagrin rushed through em. E missed the Aliyah who'd smiled, eyes glinting as they destroyed em in saira. On impulse, e put a hand on their shoulder and squeezed. They startled but didn't move away, instead allowing precious words to cross their lips.

"I do not know either," they said. "I know there is a lush forest in my dreams. I know to go there, and I know the Wagon has been… calling to me. Since it arrived and could sense me, I believe, though why or how is beyond me." They turned their intense, fathomless gaze on Rumi. "Please."

"I supposed a forest makes sense, with all that tree stuff earlier."

This time, Aliyah pressed their lips together and withheld an answer. Their hand slid under their cloak, as if to grip something there. "Will you help me find it?"

"I'll never know peace if I don't," Rumi said.

He stomped his foot down in a clear reproach at the Wagon, but there was affection in the gesture, too. Behind the curtain, a dozen metal objects fell at once. Rumi peeked and huffed as he found all of his tools, once on a metal railing, now on the table or the ground. The little inventor scurried over, hopped on the chair then bent over the table to start fixing the mess. After a moment, Horace lent him a hand. The metal tools just flew from eir hands every time e brought them near. Were those magnets? Wow, e'd almost never seen those!

Everything here was so new, so impressive, and so *thrilling*. Even without hearing the Wagon, Horace could feel it in the air around em, in the planks under eir boots. This messy haven felt safe and comfortable in a way little else ever had. Eir fingers itched with the urge to clean it up and make it even cozier, and the very thought of going back outside, in the cold evening and the market's dead silence, to face consequences for helping Aliyah escape... The void it left in eir stomach ate at em, growing ever bigger.

"I'd like to come. I—"

Horace stopped, stunned at eir own daring. Why would they care? E wasn't anything special—if anything, one could say eir failure to measure up to any standards was the only unique thing about em. But e craved this voyage, full of mysteries to solve. E wanted to be there and play more games with Aliyah, to watch them open up and find answers by their side, to build something new, without a trail of ruined apprenticeships attached to em. If e let Rumi's Wandering Wagon of Wonderful Wares leave town without em aboard, e would regret it for the rest of eir life. E had to convince them.

"I'm big and handy to have around. I can cook and sew and clean, and I've got a bit of guard training, so I know my way around a sword and shield. I promise I can make myself useful."

They stared at em. Aliyah with those impassable dark eyes, lips pinched in reflection, and Rumi with his mouth half open, his tongue flicking out for a brief instant. It felt as if even the Wagon was staring, the air still and heavy. Horace did not have it in em to wait for their verdict in silence.

"I can leave now, even! I don't have all that much here, and I swear I'll—"

"Horace," Aliyah interrupted, their gentle tone preparing them for the obvious letdown.

"Please," e pushed, desperation creeping into eir tone.

"Are you certain you want to clean?" they asked. "Look at this mess."

Surprise stole any response from em, but Rumi whirled about. "Hey! It's not so bad, I know where everything is."

Aliyah's eyebrows arched in an elegant expression of doubt, and when Rumi huffed in defeated response, their thin lips stretched into a smile. It lasted but a few sweet seconds, and Horace clung to them, trying to imprint the soft smile in eir memory. But they were saying yes, weren't they? E didn't need the memory because e'd have a chance to make thousands more. Hope swirling in eir chest, e turned to Rumi for eir final permission. He didn't seem convinced at all.

"Why do you want to leave? You have a life here, with friends and family and clan. Why ditch all that in the middle of the night?"

Shame burned through Horace, turning eir cheeks hot and red. E'd wanted a life without the weight of eir reputation, but the truth spilled out before e could reconsider. "I'm a failure here. Even my closest friends know that. I have gone through over two dozen different apprenticeships and got rejected for every single one. The entire city knows this, but I know I can be useful. Please."

Rumi's narrow eyes softened as Horace spoke, something like recognition flashing through them. His tail curled around his leg, as if Rumi was hugging himself.

"You're welcome aboard," Rumi said. The unexpected thickness to his tone vanished as he continued. "If I can't find my things, you'll hear from me. Personally, I'm more looking forward to the cooking. It's been a while since I used the burner."

Their collective gaze fell onto said burner, buried under a precarious mound of dirty dishes and instruments. Even if Rumi had wanted to use it, he'd first have to *reach it.* The sheer volume of the task Horace had volunteered for finally sank in.

"I think I have my work cut out for me," e mumbled.

Aliyah's laughter bloomed into the Wagon's cabin with a sincerity that caught them all off guard, including Aliyah themself. It had a contagious quality, this laugh, squirming into Horace's heart and expanding eir chest until e could only share it. Eir deep booming voice trumped all others, yet the counterpoint of Rumi's skittering chuckles and Aliyah's softer, melodic voice felt perfectly balanced with eirs.

All of eir life, Horace had latched on to people's laughter. Snorts and loud barks and quick and soft chuckles, e'd always found it invigorating to hear the manifestation of others' joy and amusement, a balm that could heal any hurt. Varena had once said e fell in love with others' laughter the way many fell in love with appearances.

Silly as it was, sitting in the Wagon listening to the strange music of their combined laughs, Horace knew e'd made the right decision. Perhaps e'd never found eir place in Trenaze because e had never been meant to? This would be different, e could feel it, a sense of rightness unlike anything before. This Wagon and its people were the beginning of eir last apprenticeship.

5

The Wilderness

The dome's thin film of translucent pink marked the edge of Trenaze's boundary with a clear line in the sand, and as the Wagon approached it, Horace climbed down. The entire world extended beyond this barrier, and for all of eir daydreams, e'd never expected to cross it. It felt… momentous, and Horace wanted to take the step emself, rather than to be rolled through. E should be scared—nothing would protect em from Fragments but a sentient Wagon which moved of its own volition, but only foolhardy excitement filled em, making eir fingers tingle. E passed them through the film first, as if to disrupt the energy throbbing in them, then with a jolt of thrill when nothing bad happened, strode through.

Eir confident stride faltered at the black sky and shining stars on the other side, wonder trapping eir feet to the ground. Had the sky always been so dark, and the stars so bright? E had only ever seen them through the dome, their immensity obscured by a pink glaze. The sight made em feel very small despite eir broad frame. E tore eir gaze away, but the wide expanse of the desert did nothing to diminish the feeling.

The Wagon trundled past, wooden wheels crushing pebbles under their weight.

"Hop back on, big friend," Rumi called. "You can watch from the roof, where it's safe! Fragments always avoid the Wagon."

Horace climbed back inside, used the Wagon's central ladder to reach the large wooden platform on top, and settled down, cross-legged, to soak in the scenery around em. The dirt and stone's reddish tint had turned a more muted, softer orange, with shrubs and scrawny trees tracing black lines against the ground. In the distance, e caught glimmers of gold at times, Fragment shards moving across the land in lazy patterns. None of them flew in their direction and they looked almost peaceful, a herd drifting through its natural habitat, unbothered by the strangers passing through. But the most beautiful remained the sky, with thousands of light—like crystal dust sprinkled abovehead. Horace stared at it, so absorbed e didn't notice Aliyah joining em until the blackness diminished and a blue tint crept its way through it, washing away the contrasts.

Dawn, e realized. Horace turned eastward, and for the first and perhaps last time of eir life, e watched the sun climb over Trenaze's skyline. It painted the sky in soft hues of yellow and pink and blue, highlighting the perfect spheres of Trenaze's three domes. Most of the city remained in shadows, sheltered by the bulk of the Nazrima Peak, its sharp cliffs rising like protective walls.

The city looked small—too small to have encompassed all of eir life until now, too small for the thousands that lived in it, never crossing the frontier of its shield domes. Everything still felt like a dream: the unblemished sky above, the mysterious elf whose laugh made em feel at home, even the quiet rumble of the Wagon under em, chugging away on the road and carrying em far from home, to lands unknown.

Horace gripped the hem of eir shirt, twisting it in eir fingers. E'd promised e could leave right away and glossed over any relationships e was leaving behind, but now that Trenaze was slowly growing tinier, the full weight of eir decision hit em. Varena had deserved better than a tiny scribbled note and stolen saira boards after years of friendship, tense as it could get, and after letting em hide there with Aliyah. And that was to say nothing of the others, few as they were. E'd miss Matron Dennys, who'd watched Horace grow from a stocky toddler and never lost faith in em. The bubbly elf's unwavering dedication to the twenty or so children under his care had always been a source of inspiration, and no one had been in Horace's life longer, or encouraged em to keep trying no matter what.

Dennys might have approved of this, but he'd have needed to know about it first.

Horace hoped e would return. Not now, not even anytime soon. But one day, with answers about what had happened, countless stories of the wide world, and proof that e belonged somewhere, that it had been the right choice. Along with new saira boards to bribe Varena into not murdering em instantly.

"I'm glad you're here," Aliyah said, and Horace was as startled by them breaking the silence as by the words themselves. E tore eir gaze from the fading city and offered a genial grin.

"Always good to have some muscle around."

"No, it's… it's the simplicity."

Some people would have taken that for an insult, and Aliyah must have realized because they fumbled to correct themself. Horace waved it away with a laugh.

"Don't worry, I know what you mean." Complicated sucked. E liked things better when they were simple and straightforward, and none of what had unfolded over the last day seemed to be. By comparison, the local failed apprentice must seem the most mundane, comforting thing around. "We'll try to keep things that way."

Aliyah's lips curved into a wistful smile. They set their gaze on the horizon and said no more, letting hours fill the space between them.

For once, the silence didn't weigh on Horace. E didn't itch to crowd it with stories from eir day or a good joke e'd heard earlier. With Aliyah, silence was a conversation of its own, held in their occasional smile and their relaxed posture. It was a strange feeling, to be content without words, but e enjoyed it. Something else new and unique to savour.

They stayed in companiable silence for hours, until the long immobility crept into Horace's muscles. E stretched, hopped to eir feet and jogged some circulation back into eir legs and, once satisfied most of the stiffness was gone, climbed back down into the Wagon and picked eir way through the chaos to search for Rumi.

The inventor leaned over his workbench, a

diapason in hand and glasses over his eyes, his ears close to a circular metal plate. He hit it once, listened, then hit it again. Two seconds later he slapped his tool down with a huff.

"This isn't right."

"Anything I can help with?" Horace asked.

Rumi whirled around with a startled yelp. Horace scrambled to apologize, but Rumi raised a hand and stopped em. "Blessed Inspiration, I forgot I had passengers now. No, I don't think you can help. Did you want something?"

The rebuttal left em voiceless. The friendly, upbeat inventor who'd presented Horace with a large table of creations had given way to a sharper, more anxious host, who seemed eager to be left alone again.

"Are you hungry?" Horace asked. "The desert's beautiful, but I need to move. I could put something together for all of us."

"Oh, food! You're right. I always forget food." Rumi slid down the stool. "I get very caught up. Lots of projects and all that." He punctuated that with a wave at the mess over every surface available. "Let me show you around a bit more."

Horace had never thought of emself as a particularly clean person. E had learned useful tips from several of eir Clan Viella apprenticeships, and since e'd spent years in a house full of children of all ages, e naturally picked up objects here and there to store them in a pointless battle against the hurricane of playing kids. Beyond that, though, Horace often left clothes and tools on chairs and tables, and e didn't bother with the broom very often. As long as things remained navigable...

Rumi must have a very different idea of what navigable meant. Not only did half-finished projects cover just about every surface, but cupboards, the cold box, and drawers with food and kitchen tools had no semblance of organization. Rumi's tour consisted of him opening closets or drawers, saying things like "and here we have the cutlery", only for the space to have everything except said cutlery. A bowl of fruit hid behind several jars of cereals, and prongs rested against an iron skillet in deep need of care. Somewhere deep within the cupboard were a few pots of canned beets and other vegetables, but to reach them Horace would have to fight eir way through a mess of wires, a pack of dried algae, and a scattering of forks and spoons. Easy to know how Horace would occupy eir time.

E set to work, cleaning the floor from wooden shavings before clearing out part of the counter and table by bringing everything that looked like a tool or a project closer to Rumi's workshop. This earned em a few complaints about space to work, but Horace figured the ability to properly cook would buy em forgiveness.

Humming to emself, Horace set to emptying the cupboard's shelves, placing them on the freed counter in different general piles—oils and vinegars together, oats and flour, cans or jars of pickled veggies—and then everything e couldn't easily identify. Of which there was *a lot.* E kept unearthing foodstuff e'd never even heard of. Some smelled awful, other delicious, and all of them excited em to no end. E wondered from which corner of the world they came, how someone cooked them, what they would taste like. The daydreams carried em through the work... until e dragged a linen bag from the deep end of the highest shelf, and found the most incredible thing.

"You have *dried beef*?"

E reverently withdrew one of the strips from the bag and stared at the muscle lines within it, punctuated by mouth-watering chunks of black pepper. It had to be beef, even if e'd only had glimpsed while serving at feasts reserved for the very bests, the masters of their crafts. And Rumi kept that lost in his chaos, hidden behind the rest of his cheap travel food.

"I can't believe this. Rumi!"

Horace spun around as e called out, using the full depth of eir voice, startling eir host. Rumi swivelled on his stool and pulled up his goggles.

"Yes?"

Horace brandished the strip. "Beef! Don't you know how much this is worth?"

Rumi's skittering laugh only made em pout

more, but the isixi hopped down and trudged over to gently pat eir thigh. "Almost nothing in Ardoze, my friend. Worth is relative. Over there, they'd sell you crates of it for a single pack of eggs."

That couldn't be right. Chickens only needed some shade against the hot sun and fodder to keep happy. Any city could have that, no?

"You'll see," Rumi added, "I've got some eggs stashed in the cold box, and your trash is their luxury. That's how we'll trade our way across the world. No one ever cares much about my trinkets."

He concluded with a miffed swish of his tail, then his jaw cracked into a long yawn. "I'm gonna rest. The Wagon knows the road anyway. There's an old bed stored up there, but it's the only extra I got. You'll have to figure that one out on your own. I hope Trenaze doesn't have any weird hang-ups with bed-sharing."

He dismissed the thought with a wave of his hand before slipping past his workshop's curtain. Horace stared at the point where Rumi'd last been, confused. What weird bed-sharing hang-ups could there even be?

"I doubt we fit," Aliyah said.

They were right, of course. What Rumi had called a bed was a narrow mattress with a single, thick blanket. Horace had found it stored against the wall, behind two big panes of thin iron, and e'd aired it up top for a few hours. It probably needed to stay out longer, but Horace hadn't slept overnight, and e didn't know how much longer e could stand on eir feet. Judging by the way they leaned against the upper beam for support, neither could Aliyah.

"We can. Just… not comfortably."

Aliyah's eyebrows shot up in challenge, doubts for once easy to read on their face. They did not voice them, nor did they need to. Horace would not be so easily deterred.

"I've slept buried under three toddlers before, or squeezed in with two other teenagers. This isn't *so* bad. I can lean against the wall so I don't take as much room. You lean against me, and we're good."

Aliyah conceded with a pensive grunt, then gestured for Horace to go first. E undressed down to eir underwear, then spread eir shirt against the wall, hoping to retain some of its warmth. At least the single pillow was long enough for both—Horace suspected it'd been meant as a body pillow for Rumi. Once e'd squeezed near the wall in a position to sleep, e gestured for Aliyah to join. They slipped under the blanket with only a thin shift, staying towards the edge of the mattress. There might have been an inch between them, at best, and as they shifted and shuffled to find the most comfortable position, it vanished.

Horace hoped Aliyah was comfortable. E was, but e could sleep anywhere, anytime, provided e was a little tired. And indeed, e was already slipping as the thought crossed eir mind, exhaustion catching up to em.

Aliyah's sharp elbow smacked into em, startling em awake. E gasped and found their palm on eir chest, pushing.

"No... let go," Aliyah mumbled, before

grabbing the edge of the blanket and rolling away, wrapping themself in it.

Horace froze, eir back against the now cold wall, eir chest and toes uncovered, and eir heart hammering. Aliyah settled, sleeping still, clinging to the blanket, shoulders hunched and knees brought up into a small protective ball. They seemed minuscule and frail, and Horace fought the urge to wrap eir big arms around them and bring them into a reassuring embrace. Aliyah wasn't one of the kids from home who'd run to em after nightmares. They didn't know each other, and from the way Aliyah had pushed away earlier, they needed space. Horace pushed emself harder against the wall in a pointless attempt to give them most of the bed.

E didn't sleep much that night, nor the following ones. Rest came in fits interrupted by Aliyah's frequent nightmares—which e still didn't know how to handle, or whether to mention at all—and during the early afternoon naps, when the desert heat rose to a crescendo and only the Wagon's interior remained cool enough for comfort. Aliyah never commented on the difficult nights, simply slipping out of bed every morning to climb up on the Wagon's roof platform and watch the desert go by. They kept to themself, staring wordlessly at the horizon, more closed off than Horace had seen them since they'd played saira. Meanwhile, Rumi continued tinkering. Horace, unexpectedly devoid of company, finished the necessary task of cleaning the kitchen area.

It took longer than e'd expected, in part because e'd often need to bring random junk or actual inventions to other parts of the Wagon, where e'd inevitably notice something else that needed organizing, and suddenly two hours had crept up on em, and the kitchen had barely advanced. But at least the Wagon as a whole got progressively cleaner, each surface revealed one distracted cleaning session at a time, and while the Wagon never spoke to em, it sometimes opened cupboards or drawers to help Horace find what e needed.

This wasn't what e'd had in mind when e'd

left home. Legends of inseparable heroes had floated through eir mind, sidling along the memory of a relaxed night playing saira with Aliyah and the exhilarating terror of that first encounter with Fragments. *Adventures.* Instead, e'd spent hours scrubbing a tiny kitchen or its surrounding areas, restricted to cooking simpler meals until e had proper access to the burner and cold box. But e was finished, and e had flour and water and yeast, along with perfect flatbread weather. Rumi had a brown paste he'd called hummus, the earthy taste of which would go great with the bread, and e'd found a jar of olives to add to the mix. It had been a long week, and e was no longer willing to let everyone avoid each other. Tonight, they'd have dinner together.

Horace hummed as e dove into the task, filling the Wagon with the delicious scent of yeast rising, then the sharpness of dough in a pan. Rumi peeked out of his workshop on his own, sniffing curiously, and whistled when he saw the kitchen—how he'd missed it the last few days was a mystery to Horace, but he *did* spend almost all his time in the workshop, which also had his small bed.

"Nice work," he said. "I shouldn't have doubted you the first days, when the chaos seemed to only get worse."

Aliyah climbed down from the ladder, and when they both turned their way, they shrugged. "The smell roused my hunger."

Good. Horace had been afraid e'd need to force them to sit at a table with em, but it seemed good food remained the great gatherer.

"Rumi had a deck of *Proteins* tucked inside a pot. We should spend the evening together."

"Proteins?" Aliyah repeated.

"You never played?" e asked.

Horace tilted eir head, surprised. Unlike saira, which was a local game, *Proteins* existed in various cities across the world. In Trenaze, each clan had its official set of rules, but several merchants had told em that elsewhere, rules changed with every table, as did the cards themselves, often according to which source of protein each city had most developed. The principle remained the same, however: a player played cards in front of oneself to slowly build their empire, hoarding one type of protein—poultry, beans, eggs, fish, meat, and so on—in order to increase its value. Special powers allowed players to steal or destroy their opponent's production and solidify their monopoly. Simple to learn, fun and quick to play, and many of the decks came with gorgeous illustrations.

Aliyah's only answer was a slight shake of the head, then they pointedly looked towards the fizzling pan. "It's ready."

Message received. Horace didn't press the point—e didn't want them to shut themself off even more—and picked up one of eir flattened dough, throwing it in the oil. Rumi missed Aliyah's reluctance to talk and jumped right onto the topic.

"Don't worry, I'll show you! Anyone can learn *Proteins*, and my deck doesn't have the fancier, more complicated cards I've seen around. I like it straightforward, you know? I crack my skull all day long over one invention or another, so it's no fun if I play something that has the brain melting out of my ears after. All I got that's special are these city cards you start with. They all have a power related to their respective protein, see? To give you a little boost right at the start and push you towards one strategy."

Aliyah slid into a chair while Rumi went over the rules with them, flipping example cards over to get his explanation through. Horace listened distractedly, keeping an ear out for unique rules but mostly focusing on eir bread and setting up the table. E wasn't worried about Aliyah. They'd play a turn or two and suddenly come up with the wildest card combinations and ruin them all. If anything, Horace was looking forward to it. They'd become so different, playing saira— focused but more at ease, smiling softly and preening about their cunning tactics. If e could draw that Aliyah out again, it might break them out of their shell more, and they might spend less time alone, staring, and more time cooking with Horace. Or talking, even just a little. Hopefully?

Regardless, they'd have a great evening, just the way e liked them: with food and games and good company.

Their first *Proteins* game went slowly. Horace didn't know what to expect of Rumi's deck, Aliyah played with thoughtful care, and Rumi was too busy lauding the fried bread—which was rich and married perfectly with the hummus and olives—and shoving more into his mouth to pay attention to his cards. He still won somehow, but declared it a practice round. Aliyah glanced at Horace, traces of an amused smile on their lips.

"You are right," they said. "I was not ready. But *now* I am."

Thrill fluttered through Horace's chest. E knew all too well the dangers of those words, and loved what they heralded. "Brace yourself, Rumi. We're about to get destroyed."

And indeed, Aliyah didn't play around with their next game. They had drawn Berenaze, a city nestled among gigantic trees and best known for its insects. Horace wondered how far away it stood, if their travels would take them there, and if insects were any good at all. E'd never have considered eating those, but judging by the variety of insect cards, Berenazians had learned to prepare them fried, or in pies, or dipped in chocolate or plum sauce—among many other options. Watching Aliyah play their cards made em hungry. E had gotten something more familiar: eir home city of Trenaze and its multitude of eggs and poultry options. Not that the inside knowledge of possibilities helped em at all. Aliyah built their production industry and market one carefully chosen card at a time, spending each round touching their hand one by one, eyes unfocused from the intense strategizing, before they moved to the next. Horace thought it a little strange; it was, at any rate, very different than their animated strategies with the saira board.

The reason why became apparent when they finished the game, and Rumi, whose city had been pilfered thoroughly by Aliyah in the late-game rounds, set his cards down and tapped the table with his claws.

"All right. Now do it again *without* the Wagon's help."

Aliyah leaned back into their chair. "Only if you do, too. It's not fair to Horace."

This earned them a great *harrumph* from Rumi, and his tiny tail swished in angry defeat. "All right, all right! No listening to the Wagon. I'll try, it's just—I don't even really think about it anymore? Its moods seep through and I feel its disapproval over my strategic mistakes."

"Then it will have to contain itself," Aliyah stated.

Horace looked between both of them, eir mouth hanging open as e caught on. "I can't believe you've both been cheating!"

All of eir anger fell flat at Aliyah's breezy chuckles, warmth threading itself through em. Still, e wished the Wagon would talk to em too— or send images, or impressions, or any of the things Rumi said it did.

"Think of it as the Wagon winning twice."

Aliyah picked up the cards, separated the city starters, and shuffled the rest together. "Now we begin the real count."

The dangerous edge had returned to their tone, and Horace doubted e'd stand much of a chance. Rumi must have caught the challenge there, too, as he tilted his head and tapped the table to signal he was ready to receive his city card. Horace drafted those while Aliyah finished shuffling the main deck, and then they were off.

They played half a dozen games, all but one of which Horace lost. E and Rumi quickly learned to build proper defenses for their cities—in *Proteins* as with saira, Aliyah had a vicious streak and often spent as much energy destroying other players' card combos as building their own. Rumi survived through cycling a ridiculous number of cards, using every option to draw more cards, which sometimes let him draw even *more*. Horace mostly did not survive, but that didn't diminish eir fun. Games, e thought, were a lot better when you counted your victories in the others' laughter, even if those included gleeful cackles heralding your own doom.

By the time they called it a night, Horace had filled up eir need for social interactions. Rumi had started delighting them with stories from the cities they played, filling eir mind with sweeping landscapes and a renewed taste for adventure. The days might be slower and quieter in the Wagon than in Trenaze, but e relished the freedom from expectations. No one had asked em anything, or judged how long it had taken to clean the kitchen, or how good the dinner had been. Eir two companions might need more time and space to open up than e'd want, but tonight had proven how delightful it was, to simply spend time together. The solution was easy: bigger, better meals, and countless more games to come.

6

The Dead Archives

Three mostly sleepless nights later, they arrived at the Dead Archives.

The road had sloped upward for the last few hours, a gentle rise that led them towards the Tesrima Ridge. A few plateaus jutted out of the ground, flanking it, their crumbling stone façades a lined pattern of rust and dust. The path hugged the cliff, unafraid of a deadly boulder rain, until the wall rose further up, reaching above the trail like a wave frozen in stone and time. It curled around a circular space, a giant alcove through which the packed road became a larger resting area. The transition reminded em of moving from Trenaze's open plateaus to the large cavern and the Underlake inside the Nazrima Peak.

Lines within the protected stone curve began to shine, glittering when the fiery sun rays hit them. Horace squinted against their glare until e could distinguish the crystal formations within the rock, some in natural veins while others had been carefully cut. Hundreds of glyphs emerged, painted in crystal and sunlight, their meanings long lost to time.

"Here we are," Rumi said, hands on his hips as they wheeled inside the alcove. "The first Waypoint. Unsurprisingly, we have no company."

The Wagon lurched to a full stop for the first time since leaving Trenaze, and Horace would have sworn e'd heard it sigh in relief. The absence of any golden glint from Fragment shards was almost unsettling; after days of seeing them roaming the land, Horace had grown used to their presence. Instead, the area had a large fire pit and a covered wooden box for travellers. In the depths of the alcove, where multiple glyph lines met, a cavern beckoned to Horace.

Rumours of this place had travelled to Trenaze through the rare merchant, and Horace had drunk them in. They said the inside of the Archives had once been inhabited by masters of the glyphs and writing covered every wall, carved from the very crystal they used to contain the Shield Glyph. Some thought it was a shrine to the glyphs, others talked of dark rituals and even darker secrets, the kind that predated even the Fragments. The place's history had been lost to time, as most things were, but one fact remained even today: Fragments avoided it, allowing travellers to rest for a day or two in between cities.

"It's safe, right? To walk about inside, I mean."

"Safe as can be, yeah," Rumi confirmed. "Just make sure you grab a torch if you wander through the caverns. And please get our dinner sorted first? I've got to pay our dues."

Rumi climbed down inside the Wagon, and a few minutes later emerged with an arm-full of mostly wooden trinkets he'd built either over the last few days, or before meeting them. The inventions Horace had seen in use had seemed very utilitarian—traps for animals, tools for survival, that sort of thing—but e suspected some were toys for children. E'd seen them light up and make noise, and e saw no utility for them beyond amusing young minds. Perhaps e just didn't understand, either.

Horace itched to go explore the caverns right away, but eir stomach reminded em of eir duty. E kept the meal simple tonight, using the campfire and a grill to roast the enormous mushrooms stored in Rumi's pantry, along with another round of flatbread and dried nuts. Aliyah watched em work with their usual silence, but Horace thought something felt different about them tonight. When e paid attention, e found evidence of unease in the frequent glances at the wall of glyphs and the subtle fretting at the edges of their frayed cloak. It changed the quality of their silence from focused to unsettled.

"You all right?" Horace asked, crouched near the roaring flames.

Aliyah's face was cast in shadow, but e still caught the tilt of their head—almost a shake, almost a negation.

"I am. I will be."

Their gaze returned to the glyph walls, and their whole body tensed, as if they wanted to bolt. Not exactly what Horace would define as 'all right.'

"You don't look relaxed. Is there something in the glyphs?"

Could Aliyah understand them? In Trenaze, only Clan Maera ever touched glyphs, and if they'd had any insight about the Dead Archives, it was but one more mystery to their name.

"There is power here," Aliyah said. "It lingers, untouched for centuries, but I can feel it. Maybe that is why Fragments avoid the area. Maybe they know, too."

Horace frowned. They made it sound like it was dangerous for them, and the Fragments had the right idea.

"That's why the place's safe," e said. "Power

isn't bad if it protects us, right? Like Trenaze's three domes."

Aliyah offered a small grunt of assent and settled by the fire, but their nervous jitters remained. Horace resisted eir urge to push the issue until e'd found the right words, and soon enough Rumi returned with a truly blessed gift: several thick furs and a thin travelling mattress for Horace to sleep on while they stayed here.

"The Waypoints are always full of shared offerings," he explained. "Can't take it with us, but we can sleep by the fire tonight! It's a different kind of cozy than the Wagon, you'll see."

Horace expected to collapse and notice the difference only in the pleasure of a full night of sleep. E grinned and thanked Rumi with such energy it earned em a quizzical look from Aliyah. Guilt twinge at the bottom of eir stomach. E didn't want them to know how little e slept, or that e knew of the nightmares that too often plagued them. It felt too personal, the sort of thing that quiet and reserved Aliyah would not choose to share.

"What did you leave for others?" e asked Rumi.

Rumi was more than happy to answer, steering the topic away from sleep. Horace had been right about the toys for children, which Rumi suspected would get sold at a market somewhere. He liked that, when his inventions spread even without him selling them directly— liked the idea of one day walking in a household to see a child playing with a toy he'd made, unlikely as it was. He'd also built a sort of multitool: a little box with levers and buttons, all of which brought a different tool out—knives, screwdrivers, tiny scissors, and so on. He hadn't managed to recreate it as a small, handheld version, so he'd put that one in the pile that was meant to stay at the Waypoint.

Rumi made most of the conversation over dinner, answering Horace's endless questions with relentless enthusiasm. He told of a Waypoint far north, where a volcanic chimney warmed a single cavern and countless names had been inscribed in the stones, and another in vast plains with gigantic rock formations through which the wind seemed to sing. By the time they had consumed every large cap Horace had sautéed and licked the butter off their fingers, night had fallen and e was dreaming of mysterious lands and unearthed ruins. So e picked up one of the torches left by other travellers, set it aflame in the campfire, and headed off into the Dead Archives proper, to see what wonders e could discover.

The flickering light of eir torch guided em down the initial cavern—a fairly narrow breach with a ceiling that dipped down before opening back up. Flat crystal formations lined the walls inside, as if someone had painted melted crystals rather than allowing them to grow into their usual, spikier structures. The glittering surface reflected the torchlight back in a myriad of colours, absorbed by runic patterns, briefly glowing a specific colour—some red, others blue, and yet others green or purple or orange—before vanishing. With every step, Horace brought a canvas to life, ephemeral and breathtaking, and watched it die again, its significance lost before it could be absorbed. It left em with a quiet sort of sadness, a longing for more. Eir wonder was insufficient reverence for what had once been, but neither e nor any others could truly grasp this mystery.

Horace basked in the glittering wonders, eir step slow and eir torch high as e wandered through the first cavern, into a branching path, then further down towards the one room every traveller lauded.

A gigantic cavern opened up, with three massive spires of crystal reaching upward, each its own glowing stalagmite of glyphs. They thinned near the middle, ending to a point in a beautiful swirl, then started fattening up again into a stalactite. Though shaped to resemble natural formations, Horace had no doubts the crystal had been sculpted by hand, the masterful craft proof of a talent that even those who'd achieved the highest rank—those who became *nes*—would struggle to equal. E extended eir arm to cast the torch's light as far as eir considerable height permitted and stood there, entranced by the dance of flames on crystal, the glow of words lost to the ages, and the timelessness of what remained.

"Do you have any idea what you've involved yourself with?"

The deep voice slit through the thick silence, reaching Horace without disturbing the eerie weight of the air. It didn't startle em, as if it belonged here, amongst these pillars of lost history. Only when Horace found its source—a strange figure in an orange cape and a porcelain mask, of the same heavy gait and body shape as the one who'd broken the dome shield in Trenaze—did fear gripped eir chest. The stranger stood at the edge of the torchlight, and in the dancing shadows the grin of their mask grew sinister. Horace brought the torch closer between them, as if in defence.

"The Dead Archives?" e answered.

"That is *where*." Their tone gave away nothing of their intentions. They gestured at the surrounding room in a grand sweep of their arms. "The Dead Archives, you say, as if it holds meaning to you. As if you can comprehend the markings glowing in crystal or the genius of those who left them."

"I can guess at it," Horace protested. The weight of this place had sunk into em, a reverence etched into eir bones.

"Perhaps. But we Archivists have the loss of our home carved into our soul."

"Archivists?" Horace repeated, only to be thoroughly ignored.

"You chose this path, Horace ka-Zestra," they said, a derisive inflection on eir clan rank and name, "but I do not think you are ready for it, and I'm afraid the world cannot afford another mistake."

The Archivist spread their hands out, tilting their head. The torchlight played on their mask, giving the illusion of a moving smile, a smirk, a sneer, a taunt. A challenge.

They rushed em, the cape a blur of flame in the darkness as they dashed forward. They were fast, melting into the shadows quicker than

Horace's eyes could track, deadly and impossibly graceful. Horace reflexively raised eir torch, and a blade thunked into its wood. Fear echoed through em as the sound rang in eir ears, then legs swept eirs from under em, and e hit the ground hard. In the dazed second that followed, the Archivist hit em twice, smashing their heel on eir sternum then kicking the torch away. Black noise blotted eir vision, but through the pain reverberating in eir lungs and shoulders and head, Horace still felt the cold blade against eir throat.

E blinked, and the porcelain mask was at eir ear, cold fingers wrapped around eir chin, thumb digging in. Horace dared not move.

"Go home," they whispered, deep and soft and deadly. "This is not your tale, and you will surely die for it."

Home. To Trenaze, with its three beautiful domes and quiet life, to the cacophony of roosters in the morning and Varena's laughter as e lost yet another game of saira. Home, where Horace could continue eir search for the right clan and build eir life safe from these dangerous Archivists.

Home, where e would still not belong and would return with another failure to eir name, where e would be far from Aliyah and never make them laugh again, never learn what nightmares haunted their nights or why they needed to reach this strange grove. They'd said they were glad to have Horace around, and that was enough for em. It was easy to feel insignificant, here in this grand room built by a long-lost civilization, with a mysterious and deadly adversary commanding em to vanish, but Horace had *not* chosen this adventure to abandon it. E may not be skilled, but e was stubborn and dedicated, and not so easy to get rid of.

"No."

The Archivist tensed and the dagger pressed harder against Horace's skin. E stared at the mask, at the paint where eye slits should have been, and eir voice steadied despite the panicked heartbeat.

"You're wrong. Maybe not about the dying,

but if that's my tale, then so be it. I am staying with Aliyah. Their story is *my* story."

And that was it, wasn't it? Horace hadn't come to *be* the hero. E'd come because Aliyah had needed someone, because when they had faced the Fragmented Amalgam and touched its forehead and commanded it—*your story is my story*—it had felt as if they had commanded Horace, too, reached into eir heart and touched it. E didn't belong with a clan; e belonged by Aliyah's side, through whatever came next. Eir story was their story.

Endless seconds passed and the Archivist remained atop em, unmoving, their mask concealing any reaction and withholding even their breath. They could have been a ghost if not for the cold dagger and the pain still throbbing through Horace from the brutal initial assault. Then the blade withdrew and they released Horace, and before e had even propped emself up on an elbow, the Archivist was back at the pillar's foot, the glow of the red glyphs above catching in their cape.

"Very well," they said. "We will grant you a chance. But if you want to help, heed my advice, Horace ka-Zestra: train. Train every morning atop your Wagon. Train at night, when sleep eludes you. Train with shields and swords and spears and bows, with armour or without, until you stand a chance against me. Or you will die, and so, perhaps, will the Hero."

The Hero? Horace's mouth had gone dry, from relief and confusion both. What Hero? And to do what? What did that have to do with unleashing Fragments in Trenaze? Before e could ask, however, the masked Archivist turned their head towards the entrance.

"The Fragments are awakening. They know the Hero has arrived — and so has your first test."

Then they were gone, the mask fading in the shadows. Horace opened eir mouth to protest and call after them, wherever they were, when Aliyah's fearful scream interrupted them.

Eir first test, they'd said.

E scooped up the torch and ran off.

7

The Fragments Awaken

Horace's lungs burned as e sprinted up the tunnel, towards the sound of Aliyah's scream, which had transformed into the echoes of a fight. Flickering light guided em, and strange noises bounced off the walls, distorted by the distance—moans and rattling, metal clashing, Aliyah's voice. Fear tightened eir stomach but lengthened eir every step.

A first test, the Archivist had said. Horace would not fail this one as e had so many before.

E burst into a smaller chamber, with alcoves all over the walls and a sweeping ceiling. This room had been carved, obviously so, and in its centre stood an altar of crystal shaped like an open book, its pages glowing. A single glyph shone above, its blue light casting a strange dim over the room.

Aliyah was on the other side, their back against a pillar, surrounded by terrifying, desiccated humanoids. They must have been alive once, dwarves and humans and munonoxi, but dried skin hung loosely off their crumbling limbs. Only their eyes shone, a golden yellow that could only belong to Fragments. They said the eyes of those possessed by Fragments shone like that, burning with hatred for the life that was not theirs and which they sought to steal. Horace hadn't known Fragments could take over the dead like they did the living, too, but there was a lot Horace didn't know, and none of it mattered right now.

The five creatures converged on Aliyah, arms extended. A low rattle emerged from their throats, a dry sound, the last gasps of a dying, desperate person. One lunged forward, and Aliyah swept their torch at them. Flames leaped to the creature's dry skin, but it didn't even slow, grabbing Aliyah's forearm and yanking them closer, leaning as if to offer a loving hug.

Horace stopped thinking. E barreled across the room and bodied the creature, smashing it against the nearby wall. Aliyah's torch burned hot near eir face, but e ignored it and shoved eir own into the dead human's mouth before pushing harder. It went through, crushing the skull, and the audible crack sent Horace's stomach somersaulting. E gagged but held steady; four more of these still advanced on eir friend.

Aliyah had paced away, horror etched into their dark gaze. They circled the crystal book, and all creatures followed, visibly unwilling to go over it. The things didn't seem too bright, at least. Just as Horace thought Aliyah could keep this slow rotation up while e picked them off, however, the four split into two groups.

Horace rushed one of them, grabbing a dead isixi and shoving it towards the book. It wailed as soon as it touched the altar, so Horace pressed its face into the book. The creature thrashed under eir grip, its skin crumbling under eir fingers, coming off with every lurch left or right. In its wild flailing, it clawed at Horace's cheek and chest, and e almost let go at the burning pain. Gritting eir teeth, Horace tightened eir grip with one hand and batted what e could away with the other. The creature slowed, its energy dwindling, but it left Horace's arm bloodied before it finally stopped.

E dropped the creature, panting and dazed, and turned around. Aliyah had ran another body through with hard branches, immobilizing it. Their skin had hardened over parts of their arms and face, their eyes leaking pale green light. The two creatures left jumped on their back and slammed them to the ground before they could grow roots under themselves to hold upright against the shock. Panic seized Horace, a full-body lurch that sent em stumbling forward. Aliyah whimpered under the creatures' weight, hands pressing on their chest and face, scratching at every inch available.

They weren't tearing, though. It was an urgent caress, a desperate contact, a plea borne within them for centuries—and within the rattle, Horace distinguished two broken words.

"Take... us..."

Aliyah stopped moving. A small, pained gasp escaped their lips and they reached up, fingers turning to thin branches. When they touched the two munonoxi pressing on them, a brief smile flitted over their face, the same terrifying elation they'd displayed against the Fragmented Amalgam—then Aliyah went limp under the creatures, which both sighed in relief and collapsed on top of them, hands still gently all over them. Horace stared at the almost intimate scene, horror locking all of eir muscles. What was happening? Had e failed? Was Aliyah...

Before e could complete the thought—before e could will eir muscles to move and crawl closer—a blood-curling screech ripped out of Aliyah. Their back arched, fingers scraping against the stone floor, and their body transformed further, branches growing in twisted spins around them. As if in response, the alcoves around shifted, and more of these creatures rose, moans in their throats. They did not even glance at Horace, shambling without hesitation towards Aliyah's tree body. The green light still leaked from their eyes, and sharp gasps shook their bark-covered chest, but they gave no sign of being conscious of the incoming assault.

"No..."

Horace's voice cracked. Eir arm was a bloodied, burning mess. E had no weapons to speak of, no good training to protect Aliyah... and there were so many of them. They squeezed in from the other doors, some even crawling through the top of the collapsed tunnels, skin scraping off the rocks as they did. E scrambled towards Aliyah and pushed off the two now-inert bodies on top of them before gathered Aliyah in eir arms. The branches wrapped around eir arm, solidifying eir hold, and Horace lumbered to eir feet and turned towards the exit.

A dozen of these creatures blocked the way, an impenetrable mass of bodies. Fear clawed at eir stomach, but e had no choice. E barrelled forward, a primal cry escaping eir lips as e plunged into the thick of animated Fragments, bloodied arm leading the way. Hands grabbed at

Aliyah, clutching at their clothes. E yanked them away, elbowing and punching and kicking where e could. Every step was a battle, and eir ears rang from multiple blows, from the blood pounding at eir temples, from the constant rattling of a dying, desperate breath.

"Take us... Take... us..."

Horace felt sick from adrenaline and fear and pain. The crystalline hall extended above em, and the distant dancing light of their campfire marked the exit. It was far, so far.

"Rumi!" e called, shoving through more of the creatures.

A small munonoxi with short pointed horns grabbed Aliyah's ankle, skeletal fingers clamping hard for a few seconds before the whole body collapsed with a relieved sigh. Horace's foot caught under it, shoving em dangerously off balance. E grabbed a taller corpse to right emself, but just as e pulled, Aliyah jerked in eir arms with a pained cry. Startled, Horace fell down and hit the ground hard, rolling through shrivelled legs. Branches snapped and eir hold on Aliyah loosened.

Dozens of hands replaced eirs, caressing and tugging and pulling Aliyah away. Long-dead bodies had followed them to the ground and crawled all over Horace as e desperately tried to shove them away. A hoof stomped on eir back and a small isixi tail slapped eir face. E was being trampled, and in the chaos more and more of these possessed dead shoved others away and reached Aliyah, forcing them to 'take them' and collapsing on top of them.

Horace tried to cocoon eir companion with eir own much bigger body, bearing the claws and nails ripping through em, the weight of a dozen corpses on top of eirs, crushing lungs and muscles. There were so many, active or collapsed, and more added themselves the moment they touched Aliyah. They buckled with each transfer, but the movements were growing weaker, and the thick bark skin had begun receding. The press of bodies was too much. They would both suffocate here, under this shifting pile, the stench of death filling their noses and mind long after air had stopped coming.

The pressure on Horace's back and legs lifted suddenly, air flowing back into eir lungs, a fresh burst that dizzied em. Confused, e turned over to look up. Above, piled on a shimmering platform which pinned them to the ceiling and pointlessly clawing at it, the dead still moved. The strange force field was held by five wooden rods with their metal tips stabbed into the ground all around them, glyphs shining along the pole at the tip. Rumi stood near one, both hands on a different glyph, this one etched hurriedly in the ground. It shone the same dark teal as the platform and rods.

"Come on," he said. "It's only got a few more seconds!"

Horace pushed eir sluggish mind into action, scooping up Aliyah and stumbling away. Every step sent ripples of pain through eir body, muscles and bones protesting, but e kept going.

"The Wagon will be safe," Rumi called. "Just hurry!"

So e did, ignoring the plea of eir body as e carried down the crystal-lined corridors and into the open night.

Eir steps faltered as fresh air filled eir lungs and ignited every open wound on eir body. The campfire's flame danced lazily, unaffected by the horrors Horace had just witnessed. Its light reflected on the crystal mural and the Wagon in a slow, comforting pattern. Time lost some of its meaning as e stood there, staring at the peaceful scene. If not for Aliyah's weight in eir arms and the unrelenting pain through eir body, e could have almost believed it was all a dream.

Rumi's panicked voice shattered that illusion. "Keep moving! The Wagon!"

He was sprinting out of the corridor, rods gathered in his tiny arms. Shadows moved beyond the light Rumi's sticks cast, reminding Horace that these things were nothing if not relentless. E got moving again, one stride after the other, eir grip tightening on the frail elf in eir arms, all traces of tree form gone. The Wagon lurched into movement long before they reached it, its wheels crushing rocks as it slowly headed towards the road. Horace ran up to it and, bracing for the pain, e extended a bloodied arm, grabbed the doorframe, and pulled emself in. Rumi clambered in an instant later, rods spilling on the floor.

Behind, the dead bodies slowed, confused, then crumpled to the ground. Horace glimpsed the golden light of Fragment shards above them, catching their fire's tranquil dance, then Rumi slammed the door shut and the Wagon sped away.

It was over, and Horace was alive.

It was over, and Aliyah was *also* alive.

So why couldn't e stop the frenzy of eir heart, the quick sharp breaths, the nauseating heat coursing through eir body in waves? The world had faded away, leaving nothing but eir scrambled-eggs body and its throbbing pain. E could still feel the press of dead bodies, the burning in eir lungs, the hissing voices demanding to be *taken*. E needed to—needed to calm down, to breathe, to check on Aliyah, to—to—

A small, cold hand alighted on eir thigh. "You're panicking. It's all right. Take your time. Start with the breathing, and I'll start with your wounds."

Rumi.

Rumi was here. Of course he was here. It was his Wagon. "A-Aliyah?"

"Out cold, but breathing and otherwise fine, I think. Focus on yourself, friend."

E'd saved them, partly. Despite all eir fumbling panic, e'd gotten Aliyah out of that chamber, close enough for Rumi to help. Eir first test, that Archivist had called it. Was it a success, if e'd needed Rumi? Did it matter? Aliyah was alive. E clung to the relief as e rode the aftershock of the horrible Fragment pile-on, listening to Rumi ramble on about luck and the filled water tank and bad scrapes. Something cold pressed against Horace's arm. Eir cuts burned and e yanked eir arm away.

"I can't tend to those if you fight me," Rumi chided. "You're three times my size, remember? Stay still."

This time, Rumi climbed into eir lap for better access, making it hard to focus on anything but his proximity. It helped ground Horace, and eir breathing slowed as Rumi ran a wet cloth over eir face, cleaning em like one would a baby after a meal. He worked slowly, methodically disinfecting wounds and bandaging them as he kept talking.

At first the words were like water, spilling out of Rumi's mouth and running off before Horace could grasp any of them, but as the dull buzz of panic withdrew, e managed to make meaning out of them.

The Wagon had grown agitated while Rumi replenished their water tank and went about a few repairs, alerting him before he'd even heard the first scream. He'd already had his shielding rods in hand, and he'd scrambled to come save them. From hearing it, it'd taken only a few minutes, but those had felt like two eternities to Horace.

"Thank you." The words tumbled out of eir cracked lips, rough and clumsy. E raised eir now-bandaged arm and winced in pain. It'd be a long time before e healed from this. "I don't think I'll cook tomorrow."

Rumi's skittering laugh bounced on every wall of the Wagon, perfectly at home with the creaking of the wheels. The little inventor patted eir thigh.

"I managed alone for years. I'm sure I can still make a meal."

His tail came to rest near Horace's waist, a tiny reassuring weight. The gentle pressure of it broke what little control Horace had gotten over emself.

"There were so many of them. I... they swarmed us. Swarmed Aliyah. I thought—you'd said it'd be safe—"

"It should've been!" Rumi exclaimed, frustrated. "But your dome should have been, too, and it wasn't either. And that felt like a lot of them, smashing against it before they pierced through, didn't it?"

It *had* felt like too many. Horace squeezed eir eyes shut and forced eir breaths to slow down.

The Fragments today hadn't fused, but they'd already had bodies, stolen from the dead.

"I hate to say it, but I think it's Aliyah." Rumi cast them a pointed look, and defensiveness crested through Horace, hot and pressing. Rumi raised a small hand to stop em before e could say anything. "Calm down, I'm not throwing them out. I've known something was up the moment the Wagon insisted on helping them. But if it's going to make travel this unsafe, I want to know more."

Horace pressed eir lips together. That was fair. E knew that was fair, even if e still wanted to protest. Rumi sighed and slid down from eir lap, and his tone slid back to gentle scolding.

"You've done nothing but work since you hopped aboard. Don't think I don't notice because I'm fiddling with one gadget or another! I don't want you touching chores until you've healed up some. In fact, you should go straight to sleep while the mattress is free."

Horace stared back at him as he waggled a finger at em. He reminded em so much of Matron Dennys right now, and the homesickness was too much to bear. Fat tears blurred eir vision before rolling down, and Horace wiped them hurriedly. By the glyphs, e was a mess. Nothing but raw emotions and pain, and here was this little friend, pushing some familiar love down eir throat. It made home feel so far away and yet so close all at once.

"A-all right," e managed, voice still rough. "But—"

"Of course you have a but," Rumi mumbled.

Horace's lips sealed shut, embarrassed, but eir gaze slid to Aliyah, their back propped against the wall, bruises slowly blooming across their skin where the creatures had grabbed too hard. They looked awful, and every one of their uncontrolled, jerking motions as these possessed dead had slipped into them remained burned into Horace's memory.

"Aah," Rumi said. "I'll be there when they wake up, and I'll hold off the questions if you're not around."

"Right," Horace said. "G'night, then."

And those were eir last words before e

dragged emself up to the second floor, bandages covering almost every inch of eir arms and chest, and collapsed onto the mattress, not even bothering with the blanket.

8

The Quest

Aliyah slept for four days.

The Wagon trudged on, rolling along the path
as its incline slowly but surely grew, the Tesrima
Ridge looming closer and closer. As per Rumi's
repeated orders, Horace did not cook or clean. E
did sit with a sewing kit—and discovered
Rumi's delightful needle-threader gadget—and
repaired the countless tears in eir clothes and
Aliyah's. The slow work gave em a close view on
the multiple bloodstains, but it kept eir mind
busy. Nothing but eir hands, the slow thread of
the needle, in and out, in and out. No thinking
about the rattling plea of these Fragments, which
still haunted eir nights, or of the Archivist's
promise: *you will die for this*. E almost had

already, and the conviction with which e'd accepted the possibility had vanished with its proximity.

Still. When eir gaze returned to Aliyah, to the now familiar thick ridge of their nose, the jutting bones of their cheeks, and the frail shoulders under the blanket, Horace's determination found its roots again. E missed their laugh tremendously, as if a new part of em had been ripped out. When Aliyah's dark eyes fluttered open, the strange fallow state that had overtaken Horace evaporated. E dropped the pants and sewing needle, rushing to their side.

"Good afternoon!" E didn't even need to force eir powerful cheer.

They had settled Aliyah on the two-seater and Horace had given them the only real pillow, sleeping instead on bunched up clothes. It hadn't mattered, with eir levels of exhaustion. E'd collapsed every night and woken up in a haze the following morning.

Aliyah shifted, their eyes glazed over, and Horace fought eir impatience. Seeing them move filled eir chest with glee, and it was *so hard* not to scoop them into a huge hug.

"I know you," they said, and the hesitation in their voice was a knife through Horace's heart.

"You do! We're—"

"Horace," they added.

Horace had never been happier to be cut off, and this time e couldn't resist. E wrapped a big hand around Aliyah's shoulder, pulling them up against eir chest and holding them tight, ever so briefly. Aliyah tensed for a moment, then relaxed with a broken sigh. Horace squeezed in response, and they remained like this for a long time, eir thick arms forming a protective wrap. Eventually, Aliyah wriggled out and slid farther on the bench.

"I'm glad you're awake!" Horace said.

A sad smile flitted on their lips. "So am I."

The workshop's curtain opened with a snap, and Rumi emerged wielding a wrench. He settled the goggles back on his head. "Ready to talk about this? Because I think we need to."

Aliyah closed their eyes and sighed—a long

and painful sound that emerged from deep within, dragging out so much longing and emptiness Horace yearned to bring them into another hug. Unlike Rumi, e didn't want to talk about this now. E wanted Aliyah to eat a full meal and have a moment to themself, to sort through their feelings. But even Aliyah didn't want to delay.

"You are correct, but I promise that I could not have foreseen the events at the Dead Archives. I would have warned you otherwise." They pressed their lips into a determined line and shuffled until they sat cross-legged, facing both Horace and Rumi. The rigid line of their shoulders told Horace that for all the defiant attitude, they were afraid. "I think, however, that I underestimated the dangers I pose and that you deserve to know the depths of my ignorance."

Aliyah had never struck Horace as someone particularly *ignorant*. Except perhaps when it came to casual games. E glanced at Rumi, but apart from the nervous quirk of his tail, the engineer was unreadable. Silence stretched between their trio while Aliyah carefully picked their words.

"I woke up on the outskirts of Trenaze, alone under a shelter of dusty fabric and wooden poles. I wore these clothes and cloak, and I had a bag of coins. I knew my own name. I knew the wild was dangerous, haunted by Fragments, and I knew the local language... but that was the extent of it." They brought a hand to their chest, their fingers hovering above their heart. "My only memory—if it even *is* a memory—is of a sacred grove with a giant tree, of roots and moss and stone, of branches idling in the wind and a canopy so thick it keeps the sun away. I dream of the place at night; I dream of being ripped from it. I think it's home?"

Their voice cracked, then, all matter-of-factness washed away by a cresting wave of fear. Aliyah inhaled deep and slow, wrangling themself back under control.

"That's why you wanna go find it, isn't it?" Rumi asked, his voice softer now. "You think it'll explain whatever happened."

Slowly, as if even conceding the point was a struggle, Aliyah nodded. "I don't know what I am."

Someone *did*, though. The Archivist who'd broken the shield dome in Trenaze had called Aliyah the Hero, hadn't they? They'd also knocked Horace flat on eir back in a few seconds and told em e'd die, if e stayed with them — that e'd die and might ruin everything. The sting of it remained despite Horace's bravado at the time, an echo of all the mentors who'd dismissed em and called em a failure.

"The Archivists might know," e said, eir voice rough.

They both turned to em, surprise etched in their widened eyes. "Archivists?" Rumi repeated.

"The intruder with the orange cape, the one who made the shield open? They were in there, and they called themself an Archivist. They said..." They'd said Horace wouldn't survive, but e couldn't bring emself to talk about that — to put into eir friends' heads that e'd fail here, too.

"They said the Fragments knew Aliyah was here, that they were awakening for them."

"I'm sorry," Aliyah said after a second of stunned silence.

"It's not your fault!" Horace said. "If anything—"

"No, listen to me." Their firm voice left no room for disagreement, and although the pain in it made Horace want to protest even more, e held back. "I *am* sorry, because I *am* responsible for this. These things were dormant until I woke them up."

A low rumble escaped Rumi. "So this whole awakening thing, it just follows you around? Because I promise you, the Waypoints have always been safe."

Horace bristled at the aggressive undercurrent in Rumi's tone. What was up with him? He'd seemed concerned about Aliyah's well-being before.

"Both, I think," Aliyah said. "I could feel them stirring while we ate. I wasn't sure what it was, but that shrine… it called to me, pulling me to it.

I don't even remember walking to it, only that the book was there, so close to my fingers, and I *had* to touch it, had to…" They trailed off, mouthing silent words before discarding them, searching. "*Something* needed me, and I lost myself."

"And the Wagon?" Rumi asked. "Was that how it was with it, too?"

Was that why Rumi had become so agitated? The Wagon was Rumi's entire life. He lived in it, tinkered in it, travelled in it… Would he even have welcomed them aboard, if Aliyah hadn't known about it? But what did that have to do with the Fragments? E was so lost.

Aliyah's dark eyes scanned the now-familiar wooden panelling. "To some extent. It did call to me, but it never overwhelmed me. Does it overwhelm you, then?"

They tilted their head and kept an innocent lilt to their tone, but Rumi's mouth clamped shut with a startling clack. Horace's head turned from one to the other in rapid succession, then e decided e'd had enough of feeling one step behind.

"I don't understand," e said—words e'd practised hundreds of times in eir life, of the firm opinion that e would rather ask than stay in the dark. "I thought the Wagon was already sentient. Why would you think Aliyah awakened it?"

"It changed," Rumi said, almost reluctantly. "It's more active. Anyway. I think I know the forest in your dreams. I'd had an inkling before, but all the Fragments bullshit really seals it. Only one place cursed enough for it. Wait here."

He scampered away, past the closed curtains and to his work area, shutting down any conversation about his Wagon in the process. Aliyah and Horace listened in silence as he rummaged through everything there, eventually emerging with a piece of parchment as tall as he was, all dried and cracked at the edges. Rumi unfurled it on the ground, using whatever he found close at hand—an empty pot, a rock, his wrench—to hold it down.

Inside the thick roll was a large map, detailed black lines delineating Nerezia's continents and marking its landscape. It was pragmatic, with little embellishments for landmarks, but it filled Horace with pure thrill. Maps had always been distant dreams, pretty things people set on their walls as if anyone would dare to leave the confines of the shield dome. But *this* map? This map was eir future, and eir chest grew ten times at the very idea. E flung emself on the ground besides with an excited gasp, kneeling across from Rumi.

"Is that all of it? Where are we?"

"All of it?" Rumi laughed, his tail flicking in amusement. "Not quite, I don't think. It's got my routes, but that's a lot already. The Wagon and I, we've been around. We're here."

He tapped above a symbol on the lower right corner, a pictogram similar to the curve of the stone above from the Dead Archives. Not far from it, Horace spotted the large triangle intersected by crescent arcs, a common symbol for Trenaze. The two weren't all that close, especially considering the size of their big island.

Which… really wasn't that big, once you took in the second mass of land on this map—a gigantic, sprawling mess full of symbols Horace had never seen anywhere except on Rumi's *Proteins* deck. Those few anchored em somewhat against the immensity of unknown sprawled before em. There was *so much* of the world!

"Wow," e said, and then, with childish excitement. "We're gonna be together for so long!"

This drew a cackle from Rumi. "Unfortunately, we'll all have to get used to our idiosyncracies, yes. And get a second mattress, too."

Well, that last one was certainly true. They'd be travelling for months—years, perhaps!—and Horace could only go so long without deep, comfortable sleep.

"It's not so bad," e muttered, mostly as an answer to Aliyah's inquisitive look. "So, this forest?"

Rumi tapped his claw on another spot, all the way on the bigger continent, along its northwestern edges—absolutely opposite of them. Trees *had* been drawn there—with twisted branches and next to a jagged triangle Horace knew represented Fragments.

"The whole land around there is a marsh chock-full of Fragments, but they say a cursed grove grows at its heart, nourished by the deadly shards. Never been myself, obviously. Every travelling merchant knows to make a *wide* berth around it."

Rumi punctuated the latter by tracing the trade route on the map. It didn't come even remotely close to the wasteland marked in hatching on the map. Aliyah leaned closer, perched on their seat, lips pursed.

"I would be leading you into death."

"I'm sure it's nothing the Wagon can't handle," Horace declared with utmost confidence.

The Wagon lurched to a stop. Three very long seconds passed during which none of them reacted, then Horace's gaze met Aliyah's, and laughter bubbled up their throat. They snickered, earning a scowl and a *tsk* from Rumi, and that broke what self-control Horace had left.

Eir laugh erupted in a great bellow, and e tapped the floor as if to comfort the Wagon, which creaked forward again. The crunch of its wheels turning had grown into a reassuring sound, and it eventually calmed the hysteric amusement shaking through their little group.

"We'll figure it out," Horace said when eir ribs stopped hurting long enough for em to speak.

"Yes." Rumi returned his finger to the bottom-right corner of the map, where they currently travelled, and traced their path. "First we need to get through the Tesrima Ridge using the Inari Pass, and once on the other side we can make our way down to Alleaze. That alone is a few weeks on the road."

"See? Plenty of time!" e reiterated before turning to Aliyah with an encouraging grin.

They clasped their hands in front of them, on their lap. "I suppose," they said, hesitantly, before looking at each of them in turn, and adding more heartily. "Thank you. The road may turn more dangerous than we know, and you have no obligations to me, so... thank you. I would not have wanted to be alone."

"Then you won't be," Horace said firmly. The very thought of abandoning them twisted eir guts.

Rumi stood instead, more solemn than Horace had ever seen him. His tail wrapped around one of his legs, betraying a sadness not otherwise apparent in his tone.

"Sometimes things break and go awry and it's out of your control, but you can't abandon people for that. Most days I'm a selfish little inventor living my life quietly in my Wagon, but I'm not cruel, and chasing people off when they got nothing? That's cruel."

Silence filled the space between them, heavy with everybody's worries and sadness. It was the kind of silence Horace couldn't bear, not even for a few seconds. E dropped a large hand over Rumi's head in a hopefully comforting pat before hopping back to eir feet.

"I don't think you're selfish. You came and saved us, didn't you?" And that was that, as far as e was concerned. "Let's eat! I want a celebratory dinner and some saira games."

Eir request was met with Aliyah's soft chuckles and a whispered "of course you do" — but who could blame Horace? They hadn't eaten together in days, and e hadn't properly cooked since Rumi had imposed forced rest on em. It was time to put that awful moment at the Waypoint behind them.

That night, Rumi unearthed a cache of frozen pork ribs from his cool box, and they simmered them for two hours covered in a sauce mixed from soy, sweet syrup, and pepper ground in Rumi's Self-Moving Pestle. They'd crushed nuts and baked them within cactus fruit with more of the syrup to complement the meal. Horace had always loved cooking on eir own, but doing so with Rumi was a different sort of fun: the inventor had seen hundreds of different ways to prepare these ingredients and his own overactive imagination often combined them in new ways. He said this recipe was a classic, usually with apples, but since those wouldn't survive the long trip here, the cactus fruit would work fine. It turned sweeter than they expected, but the overall meal was delicious and rich, and soon they were playing saira, wine readily served, the roughness of the Dead Archives forgotten.

It wasn't until much later that it resurfaced, as they crawled their way towards the bed, exhausted but relaxed. Aliyah stopped a foot from it, staring at the mattress in silence, shoulders tense and lips pressed into a flat line. E hated that look on them.

"I-I don't pretend to understand everything, but you know it's not just *what* you are that matters, right?" e said. When they arched interrogative eyebrows at em, Horace stumbled onward. "All I mean is, you're Aliyah, right? You're thoughtful and quiet. You learn games very fast and you have a vicious streak in them. You don't speak a lot, but when you do we know it matters. That's the *who* I got to know, and I like them a lot."

A beautiful slow smile bloomed across

Aliyah's face, and that alone was worth the embarrassment of all those words spilling out of eir lips. E grinned back and shrugged in eir best 'what? It's all true' manner. Aliyah leaned forward, touching eir forearm gently.

"This is why I was glad for your presence," they said. "You knew I turned into a strange tree creature or made Fragments vanish before I did, but all you wanted was to show me wine and saira."

Horace couldn't hold eir sheepish grin. E had wanted answers, too, for emself and the city, but Aliyah had never had those to begin with.

"We should sleep," e said.

Aliyah glanced at the mattress again and grimaced. "I fear what the night will bring."

"Don't worry, I'll have your back. Literally, if you want."

A sharp, surprised laugh escaped Aliyah, then they smiled at em, bright despite the exhaustion. "I would not mind that at all."

When they slipped into bed again, they did away with the forced space between them.

Horace still leaned against the wall, but this time e brought one arm over Aliyah, bringing them closer. For a time, eir mind drifted to eir desperate run through the possessed dead and the way Aliyah's thin frame had bucked and tensed against eir chest. E wondered how much they remembered, if anything, and if eir presence would evoke the countless bodies crushing them. But Aliyah only nestled in the space with a quiet sigh, and e felt the tension ebb from their muscles little by little until sleep found them.

Horace didn't bother pretending e understood the way of the world. All e had ever asked for was something to do with eir hands, good people to chat with, a place to belong to, and enjoyable days to fill up eir life. Despite all the failed apprenticeships and clan rejections, e'd had that, on most days—all except somewhere e belonged, truly belonged.

But here and now, as Horace held the frail dark-eyed elf a mysterious Archivist had called the Hero, e could not help but think e'd found it. E belonged at Aliyah's side. It didn't need to make sense to eir mind. E knew it with eir guts, and eir guts were the most trustable part of eir entire body. Whatever mysteries remained unsolved—whatever dangers awaited—Horace would always have one comforting certitude: eir story was their story.

THE STORY CONTINUES....

Fate and friendship brought Horace, Rumi, and Aliyah together in Rumi's Wandering Wagon of Wonderful Wares, a sentient self-propelling wagon. But their road to the coastal city of Alleaze is blocked by a flooded mountain pass — and the only person who knows how to unflood it is Keza Nesmit, the highway bandit who assaulted them the day before. Abrasive and confident, Keza makes for a thorny companion, but they'll need to work together to free the pass and continue their journey. Little do they know, this dangerous collaboration leads to secrets better left alone, and deadly consequences.

Excerpt from *FLOODED SECRETS*

Over the weeks of travel, the ground grew rougher and steeper, injecting some variety in eir daily run. They'd crossed the red sand desert to travel northward along the Tesrima Ridge, following the road up and down its slopes and making headway towards Inari Pass. According to Rumi, lush forests and a deep blue ocean waited on the other side of the stony peaks, along with the seaside city of Alleaze, where they could book passage across the water. Once the road veered deeper into the mountains, Rumi assured them the Pass itself was less than a day away. The road sometimes overlooked steep cliffs, giving Horace vertigo if e looked over the Wagon's side, or passed right under them, walls of stone blocking the sky unless e craned eir neck. When either happened, Horace let the training aside and allowed the beauty of the world to sink in.

Eir home city of Trenaze had been beautiful, in its own way. It had perched along a single craggly mountain, spread across its two plateaus and the flat ground at its foot, each section protected from Fragments by a large, pinkish dome. For the longest time, that pink had tinged the colour of the sky, and even now Horace still startled at the sheer blueness that spread over eir head. The world, for all its dangers, was full of wonders, and e wanted to see all of them.

Unfortunately, e got to see the dangers first.

They were rolling under a particularly steep cliff, the Wagon creaking its way along the narrow path. Aliyah sat on the platform watching em train as they repaired some of the many tears in their cloak. E had been holding a front stance, following a pattern of exercises Trenaze's guards had shown em, stretching eir muscles and counting seconds before switching to another, when a shadow flashed at the corner of eir vision—a flash of burnt orange dropping down. It landed in front of Horace, and e registered the thick fur of a felnexi before a wooden staff hit em—one, two, three; hip, arm, back of the knee. Pain flared through eir body and e staggered backward with a gasp, vision blurring from tears.

Aliyah jumped to their feet with an alarmed gasp, and their assailant spun on themselves in a single fluid movement, a high kick landing on Aliyah's chest and sending them flying off the platform. It happened so fast, Horace only registered it at the gut-wrenching scraping of Aliyah's body hitting the rocky ground below.

Fear bubbled through Horace and e dashed for the side of the Wagon that Aliyah had tumbled over, ignoring their assailant entirely. Which might not have been the brightest move. The felnexi stepped in eir path, grabbed eir wrist, and—despite Horace's bigger gait and weight—they pulled em forward, slid under eir body, then used Horace's momentum to roll em off their back and slam em on the platform. Air rushed out of eir lungs, and eir whole body seized in protest.

The felnexi leaned above em, sharp teeth showing from their wry smirk. "You got interesting priorities, big fella."

They had a strange rolling accent, almost like a purr. Horace didn't have enough air to answer, could only gasp as they tapped eir forehead with the staff mockingly and leaped off the back of the

Wagon. Horace dizzily contemplated the orange tail that'd vanished for a few seconds before e realized they'd gone straight to Aliyah. E crawled back up on eir knees and found the attacker with their clawed feet right at Aliyah's throat.

Preorder now at
books2read.com/floodedsecrets-nerezia

About the Author

Claudie Arseneault is an easily-enthused aromantic and asexual writer with a never-ending cycle of obsessions but an enduring love for all things cephalopod and fantasy (together or not!). She writes stories that centre platonic relationships and loves large casts and single-city settings, the most notable of which are the City of Spires series (2017-2023) and Baker Thief (2018).

In addition to her own fiction, Claudie has co-edited Common Bonds (2021), an anthology of aromantic speculative short stories. She is a founding member of The Kraken Collective, an alliance of self-publishing SFF authors, and the creator of the Aromantic and Asexual Characters Database.

Find out more at claudiearseneault.com

Other Great Books From The Kraken Collective!

If you love the mix of action and sweet queerplatonic relationship in *Awakenings*, check out *Our Bloody Pearl*, an adult fantasy in which a voiceless siren must relearn to swim with a mechanical tail under the care of a suspiciously friendly and eccentric pirate captain.

Dig into another novella lead by a non-binary protagonist and thaes close-knit group of friends with *The Shimmering Prayer of Sûkiurâq*, A deliciously queer magical person story in a secondary world with floating cities and airships, perfect for fans of She-Ra and Steven Universe.

Find all our books at
<u>www.krakencollectivebooks.com</u>

Acknowledgements

I first wrote *Awakenings* as a change of pace from Isandor—a switch from a large cast with intertwined political stories to a small, fun adventuring party that spends the vast majority of its time together. It was a breath of fresh air, a return to high magic and fun fantasy races and monsters that I needed.

So many people have helped make *Awakenings* what it is—or even make it happen at all. My first thanks *must* go to all the wonderful folks who backed the Kickstarter, putting their trust in me and my vision, and to all those who shared the campaign on social media and elsewhere. Your support has been incredible, and I am eternally grateful that so many of you believe in me this way.

Many deep thanks to my "production" team: my incredible cover artist, Eva, and equally awesome portrait artist, Vane; my team of beta readers, Cedar, Lynn, Quartzen, Al, and Danny—and in particular to Cedar here, whom I have brainstormed much of this story with, and to Lynn, who doubles as my copyeditor.

I hang about many Discord communities with whom I sprint, commiserate, share knowledge, and just generally vibe, and having these spaces has helped tremendously to stay on track and enjoy the process, with all its up-and-downs, especially as social media collapsed. There's too many people there to name, but you know who you are, and I love y'all.

Finally, but most certainly not least, I wouldn't be here without family and friends cheering me on, believing in all my new silly projects and my dreams of writing full time. I have the best people around me.

Printed in the USA
CPSIA information can be obtained
at www.ICGtesting.com
LVHW032024200224
772359LV00006B/512

9 781738 925919